Socks and Parking Places

by
Margaret P. Gregory

PublishAmerica
Baltimore

© 2006 by Margaret P. Gregory.
All rights reserved. No part of this book may be reproduced, stored in a retrieval system or transmitted in any form or by any means without the prior written permission of the publishers, except by a reviewer who may quote brief passages in a review to be printed in a newspaper, magazine or journal.

First printing

All characters appearing in this work are fictitious. Any resemblance to real persons, living or dead, is purely coincidental.

ISBN: 1-4241-4345-4
PUBLISHED BY PUBLISHAMERICA, LLLP
www.publishamerica.com
Baltimore

Printed in the United States of America

Dedicated to my husband and best friend.

Acknowledgments

Warm thanks to my soul mate and loving husband "G", who guides me daily, who is my complete strength, best friend, and my biggest fan. I know the numerous times I made you recall anguished memories weren't easy, but I couldn't do this, or anything with success, without you. To "H", my furry, golden friend and companion, who often remained at my feet during the writing of this book or would sit with me at the park and take numerous walks with me to contemplate my thoughts; and to my very dear friend, Bunny, my kindred spirit, whose long conversations are all one needs for inspiration. Your grace, brilliance, and love for literature have taught me tremendous amounts about various subjects. You were, and are, all complete inspirations and guiding lights. To all of you, I am thankful.

Author's Note

This story is a work of fiction. All characters depicted are fictional characters and are inventions of my imagination.

This novel was born from experiences in my life. Without a doubt, everyone I know and love has contributed in some way, shape, or form. If not an actual experience, then in molding me or in helping create the way I view the world. Because of the nature of this book I will only thank you and not involve you in these experiences. If you were involved, then thank you for your support and my apologies if it was not a pleasant experience. In life, unpleasant experiences can make for a good story. As I write this book, I realize the pages and pages of words—just words, but the power of words can be intense. Hopefully, the words of this book portray the power of the story behind them. Wisdom (is) the principal thing; (therefore) get wisdom: and with all thy getting get understanding. (Proverbs 4:7)

I found that in an unforgiving society it is the impossible to escape evil for an entire lifetime. I have tremendous respect for those who have had to face the evil of a lawsuit and who have had to come before, depend on, or fight the judicial system. Those of you who have been sued, degraded, and have had to fight for your innocence will understand the message of this book. To persevere, conquer, and retain sanity are only the first steps. Knowing what to do with that sanity and the knowledge gained is the second. Part of the knowledge gained is finding that, of all the emotions, betrayal has to be the worst.

FULL CIRCLE

Why is it when it appears life is being taken away or going haywire, the realization of the horrifying event may actually be the answer to a prayer? We tend to outline our lives down to the minute and when the order or the event is not according to the outline, it is often viewed as the inevitable "end" or a feeling of doom. The out of line situations that often occur may be very negative, but nevertheless it may be a form of what is prayed for, or necessary to be a revelation to the hidden strength that lies within each one of us. The life that is "waiting for us", not the one being planned, is constantly trying to rear its "ugly" head, or is it even that ugly? Time will eventually answer that question. How foolish the idea to think there is complete control to make one's own outline. When the truth be known, isn't it possible that the outline is made for each individual? One might wonder the point in even making a life outline. This never seems to be in the forefront of the mind. Not even close. Fortune and misfortune is never distributed evenly in one's lifetime, but both are necessary to learn and feel and, even more importantly, to keep perspective. Ah, perspective, could that be one of the primary principles of life? Wouldn't it be comforting, but incredibly boring if all went as planned and the controls of life's events were at our fingertips? Get a tight grip because seldom, if ever, does it happen that way.

IN THE STARS

"I see the moon, the moon sees me," were the soft timid words being sung as the tiny fingers patted the dog's tummy. Jory and Friskie were lying on the steamy sidewalk on their small cozy farm located in the heartland of Kansas, staring at the day lit moon. The moving clouds caused Jory to giggle and discuss the Disney figures, spaceships, and the multiple figures displayed by the clouds. This afternoon delight, of course, was the furthest thought from the young child playing with his Lincoln logs in dusty western Kansas. Living separate lives and hundreds of miles apart gave the stars ample time to line these two intertwined lives together.

The snowy blonde hair on Jory Mann's four-year-old head grew whiter and whiter until it resembled the synthetic look of a doll with each passing summer as a result of the time she spent playing outdoors on her farm. The farm brought a whole playground to her fingertips. Often, she was forced to play by herself when she couldn't successfully recruit a playmate. In the end, this taught her independence and helped expand her imagination. She never wanted for anything most of the time, anyway. She wasn't a child with many material items or store bought toys because she owned the world with the zoo and playground in her own yard. It wasn't just a "back yard", but acres of fruit trees, which offered natural snacks if she got hungry while climbing them. The trees, alone, could keep a child busy for hours with the tree houses and the tire swing appendages. The old rundown buildings converted to forts in times of need for she and her sibling soldiers. And then there was the barn. The barn wasn't an ordinary barn, but a homemade, old, huge, red barn her grandfather had built. It had hay to play hide and seek, a huge rope with a tied knot that could hold her while she swung like a monkey between haystacks. Maybe the most fun was the secret floor "windows" in the loft that she could drop down through to the bottom floor of the barn without ever going outside. She absolutely loved those.

It took many years to fully appreciate the fact that the outdoors turned out to be her best friend as she never strolled around the farm without her furry companions, whether a dog or a cat or any other four legged beast. Farms were hard on animals, but she always had a furry friend by her side. Little did she know the love of animals would follow her for her entire life. Cats never won in the popularity contest because they just didn't stay around long enough. It was too hard on Jory to get close to a cat and then have to go through losing it. She learned to keep her distance to most of the adult cats as her defense mechanism. The kitties still won her over unknown to her that they were the most vulnerable to the menacing elements of the farm. The last straw in distancing herself from cats was with her cat "Smoky", who almost died dangling from a fishhook that was left on the front porch by her orneriest older brother, Joe. It was about all Jory could handle as she watched the cat dangle from the hook that was attached to its poor, helpless, furry neck. Fortunately, multiple siblings came to the rescue or, to some, the adventure.

It was her small life and she liked having it all encircled and together. Her childhood continued to offer independence and creativity. She grew to attend a small, quaint country school about one mile from her home with an average class size of about five. It gave her great comfort that she could see her farm from school and school from her farm, although not as much with the latter. She often played softball in her front yard since it was as big as a ball diamond and her family was big enough to support two teams. Of course it had to be the boys against the girls. She loved to swim at the nearby county lake or farm pond with her siblings. Horses were her big, furry friends and how she loved to ride. Pepper, her very own horse, often transported her to the lake or pond and usually not without incident. Another favorite pastime was being pulled behind a truck on the remains of her brother's makeshift dune buggy especially in the middle of winter on the snow. The possibilities of adventure on her farm were endless.

She was allowed to drive old trucks out in the wheat fields by the ripe old age of eight, which progressed to filling up the cars with gas, all by herself at the age of ten. Filling vehicles up with gas was more of a responsibility because it required driving the auto up to the shed and lining up the gas tank with the nozzle. The whole distance was probably equal to a city block. At any rate, it offered a feeling of great independence and it was way more fun than pretending to be driving a car. It was an interesting childhood and offered many aspects and views to life.

She felt her life ended when she was in seventh grade and her parents told her they were selling the farm and moving west to some unknown little southwestern town in Kansas. She was devastated. She had just entered the "real" world of junior high with much success. She got off the farm daily to become a friend to many, a cheerleader, a junior high queen and one happy teenager with her new world. Her acceptance was unfamiliar to her, but she thoroughly enjoyed it. That would all soon be ending, or so she feared. What could possibly be good about moving to a small southwestern town?

Screeching and swerving on his bike to miss his younger sister, Mason Gray arrived at his home, panting, out of breath, and boyishly excited. He ran to show his mom what he had designed and built for the neighborhood on Clay Street. Mason continued to play and build every imaginary piece of equipment known to a small child with the

Lincoln logs until he moved on to the more complex erector sets. He cloned families of robots until he got old enough to actually build with real materials. He had become the neighborhood engineer in masterminding his new idea of the biggest, baddest tree fort known to all *small* men. Mason was an independent child and was extremely creative. He was the cutest little boy, with the softest warm curls and a fairly small body frame. He had an enormous imagination. He was what one would imagine as a "little Einstein" mentality wise, but would definitely include "absolutely adorable" in the description. He was the type of child who, when you looked at him, had the capability to warm your heart by just watching his energy.

    He, like other children, maybe even children in the heartland of Kansas, loved his animals, especially "Red", his Irish setter. He loved riding bikes and playing sports throughout his childhood years. One of his favorite pastimes, when he wasn't building, was to go across the neighborhood and lay in the large sunflower field to fly his kite. He enjoyed solemn time to himself. As he grew and entered junior high his entire life changed. He proved himself to be extremely athletic, a fun all-around good friend to many and especially to his lifelong buddy, Seth Seagal. Seth and Mason met when Mason was five and the two played together whenever possible. They were inseparable. Surrounded by friends, Mason still preferred to be his own creative person and spend as much time as he could, involved in his own created projects. He was, however, beginning to find out he did enjoy the relationships he was developing in junior high school and just maybe girls weren't as bad as he and Seth had previously thought. With their combined intelligence they had numerous unproven theories about the young girls in their lives—could they have been wrong?

MASON AND JORY

    Splash! Sparkling, glistening droplets fell one after the other frolicking into one humongous tidal wave. This was the repetitive scene of the momentous day! In went Jory Mann with a forceful cannonball. The county fair dunking booth was a tradition and a way to raise money for high school activities in the small western town of Liberal, Kansas. The dunking booth didn't look like it would turn out to be something Jory would normally enjoy. Watery sprays emitted from the unleashing of the dunking board following each cannon ball that Jory performed. Mason Gray was the perpetrator of the fast balls that unhinged the dunking board, sending Jory straight into the frigid water. Underwater, the freely floating, giggly high school demoiselle had butterflies in her stomach from knowing that her best friend and boyfriend had thrown that bullet of a ball. Jory believed that "bullet" was her fate to becoming Jory Gray. This was a memory that always brought a warm smile to Jory.
    Prior to marrying young, they had known each other since the end of their junior high years. They met after Jory was forced to move to the dreaded western Kansas town. Now, after successfully being

married over a decade, Mason and Jory Gray continued to be a couple many admired.

Mason, a young thirty-one, was the good looking, all-around American guy who everyone adored. A feisty, athletic young man with curly dark hair, hazel eyes, and still had his warm smile and an amazingly intelligent mind. He successfully carried that trait with him since his childhood. His smooth, tanned face displayed strength and distinction and continuously emitted warmth. The hazel eyes opened up to a soft heart that revealed his gentleness and patience. His physical strength was beyond belief, not an ounce of fat on him, but his muscles were as defined as a geological map. Jory nicknamed him "Tank" to help define his strength. Mason had a calming way about him that when he spoke, people listened. He was determined to be a millionaire by thirty. So far, he had not met his millionaire goal. As an engineer, which next to Jory was his life, lived by the theory that measurements were close enough if the result was plus or minus ten percent, so to Mason, his millionaire goal, based on age and not money, was still a viable goal.

Jory, thirty years old, was a tall, beautiful brunette with matching brown eyes and was equally intelligent. She had fallen in love with Mason in high school. Love at such an early age was often questioned, but the years had proven it to be a true love. Her high energy, non-calming ways were quite opposite of Mason's, but still they were totally compatible. Unlike Mason, when she spoke it was fast and from one point to another. This was a remnant of her challenging childhood being second to the youngest of five assorted siblings. Growing up, whenever she spoke or tried to get her story told. Interruptions were constant, with nobody listening and she grew to appreciate anyone who *would* listen.

People that knew Jory felt she had a gift. One of the nicest compliments she was ever given was the question asked by a friend, "Does everything you touch turn to gold?" She never felt that she had a gift, but hoped that it was true. She hated to think she was just filler.

Through many years of growing as classmates, friends, school outing buddies, county fair dates, falling in love, becoming boyfriend and girlfriend, losing virginity, a couple of years of college, Mason and Jory married young. Before they got married, they had been separated by attending different universities. They both endured temptations, but overall felt a void that only each other could fill. They had argued and fought most of their separated time, both learning they couldn't live without each other. They had sound morals, albeit a few stumblings, but living together was not an option until they were married.

    They spent their first married years together in college and trying to get established as a married couple. Their schooling continued for many, many, many years until both had earned two degrees each. The paths they traveled paralleled each other every step of the way. A book stuck between them was a part of their daily routine. Whether it was on the couch together or sprawled out on the bed there were always books; textbooks, reference books, engineering books, pharmacy books, journals, you name it. Not to say intimacy couldn't be accomplished, and well appreciated. It may be on the book, by the book or the book ending up on the floor or over the book, but somehow there was a way.

    The two of them always knew, knowing each other for such a long time was the true key to their success. Ending up together was truly the inevitable for Mason and Jory. Intimate lovers and soul mates came as natural as the morning sunrise. They wished other people; especially couples could understand this process. Their relationship, their history together, how it worked and their deep friendship turned out to be the best-kept secret of all. It was obvious that many couples never had the fortunate opportunity for this type of intimate relationship. This was a puzzling issue. Jory often wondered why she and Mase were blessed with this amazing relationship.

    When Jory was twenty-two, she became very ill and learned she was unable to have children. At that point in time, Mason and Jory decided to be free and live life to the fullest by whatever life had to offer even though they had always shared the idea that if they would have any children they would have a minimum of seven. Joking, to some degree, a party of children under one house was beneficial for the children as well as the parents. Not having any children had never occurred to them, but the news of possibly being childless would not be an obstacle for them. It would be an opportunity. This was their philosophy in life more times than not. All around good attitudes would bring good life. Jory felt this, as well as their life together, was a gift from God. "Do with it as one may."

Dr. Goldstein, the surgeon who performed the partial hysterectomy, explained the news to Mason and Jory about not being able to have children. The IUD had caused extreme damage which forced him to do a partial hysterectomy, but fortunately he was able to save one ovary and one fallopian tube. By saving the one side he explained there may be a chance to conceive a child if they tried, immediately. It would have to be immediate since the remaining ovary and tube were open and clear from the surgery. In a short amount of time scar tissue would more than likely block the fallopian tube, making it impossible to conceive. Jory, after coming out of the long but healing surgery, was joking and taking the "conceive now" statement literally. She was still elated knowing she was now well after months of suffering, she excitedly spurted out, "NOW isn't a good time, considering I just got out from under a knife!"

Mason using persuasion and joking with her, said, "Trying would be fine, in fact, actually welcomed." He spoke ornery in his soft voice with a very warm smile. Turning serious and explaining intelligently, he said, "Jory, I think we should wait. Just because now is the time, medically, it really should be more of a commitment than that."

After hours of discussing the right of a child having a "right timing" component the issue was decided. Both evaluated the news scientifically and emotionally and decided it would not be allowed to hurt them. Whatever would happen would happen. They would live their lives normally and forget all forms of birth control. Birth control had not been a friend to Jory, first a blood clot and now this. She just wanted good health and she wasn't getting it from external methods of birth control. Jory believed God had his reasons and obviously a different plan for them from the "ordinary." Mason and Jory's closeness was only enhanced by the news. Unknown at this point, throughout their life this issue would be a point of contention with many and very misunderstood to almost everyone they met.

    If there was a dark side to the news, it was in the back of Jory's mind. From the ordeal of a major surgery there was a down time in which she felt sad. Thinking about all aspects of this news she felt it might be God's way of letting her know she would be somewhat less than a good mother. She had very little respect for her mother's display of affection for her children and somehow Jory feared she would be equally as bad or worse due to history and genetics. Something along the lines of, "The sins of the father" concept haunted her. Or in this case it was, "The sins of the mother." Although, both cases really applied. Obviously, the behavior of her mother did affect her greatly. After all, isn't that how it worked? Jory was grief-stricken by her family upon numerous occasions. By today's standards, it would have been viewed as a fortunate family, a mother, a father, and five children all under one roof. "Ideal? No." There weren't any beatings or physical abuse, but still dysfunctional in one of the worst ways—a pessimistic mother who insisted on looking like a close family—at any cost. A selfish woman who hid behind good deeds for self gain and used distorted values as her basis. Her skewed ideas were made to fit her lifestyle. Creeds, creeds, creeds, convictions, convictions, convictions, but all void of any character. The feeling of others was not a concept to her. Jory was never fooled. Love and compassion were absent, unless it was for personal gain. In Jory's adult life, it bothered her that she couldn't remember a time her parents were concerned about her that didn't somehow affect their own self gain. When she told them she had been very sick for months and had finally found a warm, gentle, intelligent doctor to help her as she presented all the specifics to her parents their concern was that it was going to interfere with their plans and was it *really* necessary. Trying to avoid these dark thoughts, she couldn't help but notice, except for Mason and her brother, Jeff, there wasn't going to be any other family that came to visit her during this ordeal. To her this was a big deal. She felt this one. Upon numerous occasions, it bothered Jory immensely how one could not escape genetics. No matter what she would do in her life she knew she would never be able to do anything about her genetics and God knows she tried her entire life.

All through these trials, college still remained a big part of their life. Mason had acquired a Master's degree in Mechanical Engineering and had a true knowledge and talent in robotics.

Mason knew how to acquire patents faster than they could be printed. His past few years, working as a Design engineer in Austin, Texas, had proven his engineering was a God given ability. Engineering was second nature for Mason. Jory was a horticulturist by interest and from her first degree. She changed directions and pursued a pharmacy degree. An atypical mixture of education for Jory, but she was a naturalist, she loved nature, animals, trees and had a deep interest in medicinal plants, which led her to the chemicals of pharmacy. She had enrolled to study for a master's degree in horticulture to work at a pharmaceutical company making medicines from plants, but switched gears and decided to get paid better by getting a pharmacy degree. The end paths for both degrees would lead to the same place, but with enormous differences in pay. Amazing how the wording on a diploma could make such a financial difference. Jory, excited about her upcoming graduation from pharmacy school, could see the incredible opportunities for both her and Mason. She loved what she saw.

One more eternity month, that's all just one more, seven hundred twenty hours, forty three thousand two hundred minutes and I'm outta here—Aaugh, Jory thought as she did her daily, calendar, arithmetic. The balmy, gray November morning was precluding the long-awaited Pharmacy Commencement at the University of Texas. It was just another day as Jory marched uniformly through the large glass doors to Malott Hall, for a seminar on Pharmacy Automation. *Seminars, SHIMINAR. Geez, when will this be over?* Jory whined the sarcastic thoughts for the repetitious morning. Jory was just finishing her last lecture series on the malignant topic of chemotherapy. From the first day of classes, this horrible subject had its own ominous hovering over the classroom. Jory had own concept on chemotherapy, not without intelligence and a great deal of thought. She had come from oblivion to knowledge on the subject and was awestruck on the accepted regimens of chemotherapy. No doubt technology was making great strides, but current methods seemed skewed. Jory immediately figured out there were some things in life one was better off not knowing. She often evaluated the "ignorance is bliss" theory as being a true blessing for many of life's topics. This was an area of pharmacy that terrified her. Her grandparents had died painful, drawn-out deaths. Mother, aunts, and sisters still fighting their own battles. So far they were successful in fighting the cancer, but not the fear. She often fell back to the old saying that fear, in itself, had torment. She tried hard to avoid fear and to have faith; however, the dark cloud of illness tried to hang over her for her entire adult life, but she did live with an attitude that she would never let it catch her. "I'm going to run faster than it can," she would often say, and jokingly, but at the same time she was dead serious, though slightly fearful. The genetic factor had once again haunted her. Whether it was subconscious or not, she believed in positive thinking and the power it possessed. The intensity and the power of the chemo drugs intrigued her, but frightened her even more, knowing that a single entity could have the power to heal or kill. Unknown to so many that the latter more likely, but prolonged. This was the big secret that the medical community kept from cancer victims. The victim felt healed from the treatments, when, in fact, the treatment prolonged the cells from reappearing for a period of time. Maybe this presentation was not a bad thing, but either way, it was disturbing and amazing, yet fear-inspiring. The science of it all seemed so backwards to Jory. She wondered many times, *Why doesn't common sense take over these medical professionals?* They knock the immune system out instead of building it up with these treatments. Her instincts told her that some day chemotherapy would be as far off track as blood letting was in the eighteen hundreds, but still a stepping-stone to gaining the knowledge needed. She believed in preventative medicine, but, like with so many areas in our society, had it been taken to the extreme? She often thought, *Go ahead and get rid of the tumor, but let people live.* Jory came back to the moment at hand only to realize she was about late to her next lecture.

Upon numerous occasions, Jory would lapse into these heavy evaluations of certain topics. The pharmaceutical enlightenment thrilled her because she was content knowing her career was an area she enjoyed and it had substance. She was a big believer in life's offerings having substance. Jory settled into thinking, *Another hour lecture and one hour closer to graduating, seven hundred and nineteen and counting.*

Several of Jory's friends had entered the lecture hall, mumbling about everything that was of little importance in the world as the distinguished pharmacist from the Veterans Administration was being introduced by Professor Malone as the guest speaker. Jory preoccupied with all of her scheduling for the next week constantly placed dates on her calendar, scratching out and adding something to every day as she was always planning and replanning. She would double check the days, hours and minutes until graduation just in case she overlooked a major amount of time. Disappointed, the length of time until graduation remained a constant in spite of all the additions or deletions made to her calendar. If it was on her calendar then it was history in the making. Suddenly, she hears a statement that struck her like a bolt of lightening and unknowingly it had the potential to change the rest of her life.

The guest speaker spilled out a statement, "If our VA had automation today we would buy it. We just can't find it." It was a well known fact that pharmacists were typically overworked, misunderstood in what they did and inundated with mundane tasks that took such valuable time away from the more important tasks. These important tasks were the tasks that Jory lived for in her upcoming career. The building of a rapport with her patients by educating them on the proper use of their medication, improving their quality of life by getting them involved in their own health care and counseling each and every one of them. Currently, pharmacists complained this was next to impossible with current methods.

Jory was awed by the statement that no one had helped out this poor agency. "What, all this money to be spent and nobody to help them?" To Jory, automation and technology was becoming old hat after hearing about it day in and day out from Mason. As much as Mason talked and lived automation, the topic itself was automated. "What does this man mean—if he had automation?" Jory knew exactly who could do this for them. Quietly she muttered under her breath, "Wait a minute, mister, have I got the guy for you!" Without any thought at all, she fidgeted through the rest of the lecture and then jumped out of her seat to call Mason. "Mason, are you sitting down? Wait till you hear this!" Destiny was in the making.

Jory returned home and immediately slipped into her one and only black satin teddy. Jory could be very spontaneous and full of surprises, but it didn't happen often since her pharmacy studies had completely consumed her life for the past three years. She wasn't proud of this fact, just a result of infatuation and a means to an end. She knew it had affected her and Mason. Perhaps, Mason more because Jory selfishly let herself become consumed by her studies. She should have been the master of selfish ways since this was her childhood teaching. She often wondered if there was a more selfish family than her own. She wasn't proud of it, but her selfish ways lately had become a defense mechanism to help her complete pharmacy school. Jory was constantly becoming more excited about the direction and the accomplishments of her and Mason's life. She knew Mason would be home in fifteen minutes. Quickly, she found her and Mason's favorite romantic CD. The lights were low and George Winston was in his "Summer" season playing, "Living Without You." Jory slipped into the back bedroom only after she prepared and dropped a little pink note trail across the entry way, into the living room and leading into the back bedroom. There Mason would find her lying beautifully and willingly waiting for him. Her sensuous body was a warm rosy red, her long, silky brunette hair was shining resting on her baring shoulders and her smile was absorbing.

Mason had come through the front door. "Jory," he said with a Doppler effect in his voice as he figured out what was ahead of him. He did exactly as he was instructed and followed the notes to the welcomed destination. Mason immediately swept her into his arms as she began to remove his tie and unbutton his shirt kissing each newly exposed area. He slid down the black spaghetti straps, brushing her silky strands of hair behind her shoulders and began to feel her soft voluptuous breasts kissing her entire body as it became exposed. The scent of her soft, subtle fragrance covered her body from head to toe. The aroma euphoria, alone, was experienced from smelling her hair and continued down her entire body. Mason loved the way Jory's hair smelled. He could become aroused from her scent. Quickly, all clothes occupied the floor. They became totally absorbed into each other as one. They made love until late into the evening. The Champaign that had been chilled and bubbly by the bedside had lost all its fizz and chill, but neither noticed or cared. The warmth and love could not be bothered by such minuscule details. Mason and Jory laughed and planned their future the rest of the night, knowing nothing could stand in their way. As the dark of the night approached, both fell fast asleep in each other's arms, appreciating the peaceful sleep.

THE LITTLE APPLE

A Ford Mustang had been limping along for several years and had left the two stranded for the last time. Jory joked that her thigh had been shown for the very last time, except to Mason. "This thigh is officially retired, no more begging for rides."

With all of the changes that were about to take place in their lives and a promising new future ahead of them, Mason and Jory finally purchased a new vehicle. "Credit!" she exclaimed. "Ain't it wonderful?" They both knew this was their way to get started. After all, it was "The American Way."

The new, sparkling Champaign-colored Trooper had no room to spare, not even for a Texas fly to move back to Kansas with them. December eighteenth was a typical Texas December day, where the temperature was a cool, crisp sixty degrees and sunny. To a non-Texan, the weather made Christmas seem as far away as the threat of snow. Snow just didn't exist in Austin, but it could rain harder than one could imagine. The rains had an attitude with an intensity that lasted for hours, never taking a breath. Above the smog of the city, another lingering planet of enormous translucent skies existed. The natives of Austin, Texas, never knew a horizon without smog or the magical transitions of new seasons. To not experience the freshness of a new spring with newly bulging buds anxiously awaiting their time to beautify the world, storming into the warmth and balminess of summer, which eventually cooled right into the magical fall colors, to remind the world of a complete life cycle bringing on one of Jory's favorite cold and beautiful snows, was completely unheard of to Jory. Mason and Jory were looking forward to returning to those gorgeous, Kansas seasons and skies. Smog was non-existent in most of the state of Kansas. The cities were too small, most only having room for the local bar or gas station. The sunsets were a true experience of life. A collage of every existing vivid color blended together. The kind of sunset one could feel God's presence in the paintings of colors, inexpressibly beautiful.

It felt good to see the Texas highway diminish to a "v" in the rear view mirror. The one true sadness was to leave their two dear friends, Dan and Linda Parks. The four of them had been friends the entire time Mason and Jory lived in Austin. Dan and Linda were the kind of friends one knew would be a lasting friendship, no matter how much time passed in between visits. Nevertheless, there was a loss, and sadness to part. Texas had been good to Mason and Jory. There was a saying that "Texas was a whole different country." This was actually an understatement. It definitely was a whole different country, but it served its purpose. Now it was time to return home—to their real home, in their own country.

The excitement escalated as the Trooper danced the winding roads through the Flint Hills of eastern Kansas. After several hours of driving through the sparsely decorated countryside of northern Texas and through the entire red dusty state of Oklahoma, the dancing Trooper was picking up it's step and was entering the densely tree-covered Flint Hills that owned the quaint, collegiate town of Manhattan, Kansas, known as the "Little Apple." Manhattan was Mason and Jory's favorite place. This is where they wanted their home to be. After months of struggling and pondering on where they should make their permanent home it was decided Jory could work anywhere. Mason owning his own company would allow him to be able to work out of anywhere because he would have to travel everywhere. Manhattan offered an airport that had a commuter airline and Mason had acquired his private pilot's license while in college so he could travel in a private plane, too. To continue pursuing that avenue would not be a disappointment to Mason because he loved to fly. After both of them completed their first degrees from Kansas State University, both were extremely sad to leave the warm, friendly town of Manhattan. Both believed they would never have the opportunity to return to Manhattan due to the size and the economy. To many, the small town wouldn't seem glamorous enough, but to these two it had a special meaning and it was ideal. The big city life had its great times, but this is where they wanted to be more than anywhere. Their long-awaited dream was finally coming true. Jory looked at Mason and shared the biggest, warmest smile they had shared in awhile. With all the hustle and bustle of graduation and moving, tensions and pressures were high, but the excitement of this new life erased those anxieties.

Mason found the long trip a great opportunity to plan his new venture. He tossed thoughts back and forth in his mind like a ping-pong game. Finally, the gray matter grew fatigued. Mason often drifted into his own creative world and produced amazing results. Jory knew she had the potential to rattle on and on. Mason's array of smiles convinced her that much of it was not heard, much of the time. It didn't matter as long as they both understood when to listen and when to be quiet. Both these qualities took some time to master, but in time both eventually succeeded, most of the time. Mason's flow charted mental images included massive quantities of information. *How was he going to get started? How was he going to support him and Jory in the infancy stage? Would Jory's job be enough support financially? Did he have what it took to do any of this? Was he going to start a company or sell an idea?* The more he thought, the more the adrenaline rushed like a newly formed rapid in a gorging river. He suddenly realized a considerable amount of time and countryside had passed and he hadn't noticed either. What was Jory talking about? She had been singing to the radio last time he checked, but she had advanced to voicing her unwarranted concerns about what kind of pharmacist she was going to make? Neither her or her new job had any idea she aced her state boards, something very few accomplished. She had been told a hundred percent was never accomplished. In fact, it wasn't even attainable as far as she knew. The thought of her making a hundred percent never entered her mind. When she took the licensing boards to become a pharmacist, after all her years of schooling and months of studying for the exam, she became ill the day of the exam. Her fever was one hundred and two degrees and her throat felt like someone had used steel wool on it. She couldn't remember feeling this bad in a very long time. Somehow it turned out for the best. The illness made her care less about the exam and in some odd way, had a relaxing element to it. She went into the exam with two goals, one to finish and pass, and two to not die trying. She was bordering on delirium. Just passing was actually all she prayed for, not knowing her congratulatory letter awaited her with the one hundred percent printed on it. It was a habit for Jory to short change herself on her God given abilities. She constantly underestimated her actual capabilities. This was all in part to her upbringing. There was no recollection of anyone in her family trying to push her to success or letting her know she could do anything she put her mind to. She figured it out on her own and with Mason's constant support. She didn't tell many people that she was in pharmacy school until her last year. School was a means to an end, not something she wanted to do. School was hard enough without any additional negativity mixed in. She usually did accomplish what she set out to do. She found irony in the fact that it really was that easy. Believing was ninety nine percent of the battle.

Both Jory and her new job awaited the news of whether she was a registered pharmacist in Kansas or not. Jory had been hired by Dillon's Pharmacy, a chain supermarket, pharmacy. She would be a staff pharmacist making eighty thousand dollars a year. This was unthinkable to her that she was going to get paid well for something she loved to do. This had such potential for being fun. Fun was good and long-awaited. Amazingly, Jory never really let the financial end interest her much when it came to pharmacy as a career. Pharmacy was just what she truly wanted to do. She was so thankful to find something that interested her this much. Worries of being seventy years old and never doing what she wanted did concern her from time to time until she found the world of pharmacy. It was a big deal to Jory to live life with few regrets. She knew many, many people who never had the luxury of finding their niche in life. She disliked the bitterness these people would show for their lack of finding their true love in life's offerings. Mason never doubted she would make an incredible pharmacist. Jory not only had the intelligence, but she also was a warm, compassionate person. She had a knack for taking a person that didn't feel well and turning them towards, at a minimum, hopeful. Mason loved this quality about her. He loved how close they were and that there goals were aligned. When she would plaster him with one of her warm smiles and those big brown eyes, he would think he was having a heart problem. He felt as if his heart was in an arrhythmia, or as most know the feeling, "flip-flops." Jory would mistakenly think he wasn't listening when, in fact, he had lost all concentration admiring her when she would talk with him.

After two days on the road, Mason and Jory pulled up to their new home. The excitement of this moment was overwhelming. Here it was, there cozy, yellow limestone, two-story home—123 A.J. Fritz. Even something about the address seemed configured by some master engineer, to make it so simple.

TROUBLE

Matt Coggins placed his right palm against the palm print scanner before entering his accounting firm. He made sure he and his staff used only the latest, most expensive, state of the art equipment. It wasn't even an option to have anything less than the most expensive, latest gadgets for his staff. It didn't matter if it was the best, but it had to be the latest, most expensive, state of the art, equipment.

The high-tech computer began to blink and beep, communicating competently, as Derrik Peters entered his plush, secure office. This was a daily occurrence and Derrik understood the importance of these messages. Derrik was Matt's right hand man. Many had referred to him as Matt's robot or "yes" man. Derrik was pretty much incapable of anything that took an extreme amount of thought, but he could lie, cheat, and steal among the best. Derrik went to his state of the art computer, pulled up the encrypted screen, on his secure line, which was possessed with only binary signs and symbols that no one would be able to understand except the special PGP software. Matt was extremely paranoid and if anything in his life could be encrypted then it would be encrypted. If there would have been a need for him to encrypt his address he would have had it done. Derrik had to enter his security key to begin the decryption. He downloaded the message to his flash drive. He deleted the encrypted message off the screen and changed to his pocket PC. After a few seconds, a spewing of paper appeared, very quietly from the wireless laser printer—the message, decrypted. The message read: *Derrik keep a low profile. Let's continue the day-to-day operations of our current business and hold off on "acquiring" any new. The perfect opportunity will come along again and the timing will be optimum. I have enough going on right now starting these companies and arranging the books accordingly. Remember, diversifying is the name of the game. To set these companies up so they fail and go into Chapter 11 is taking much of my time.*

Susan, Matt's wife, one of the CPA partners and a bankruptcy accountant, acted as the accountant in Matt's set-ups and prepared all the final paperwork for him.

Oh, just a reminder, make sure you delete this message off of any hard drive. I know you know to do this, but we just can't be too careful. Our two friends will be willing and ready to "invest" when we give them the final word. They remain our umbrella. At the present time, they are in Puerto Rico on stand-by.

Signing off—The Equestrian

Derrik, nervously gathered the papers, shredded them and tucked his flash drive into his pocket. He was used to this procedure and he knew how to take Matt's commands and responded accordingly.

Matt Coggins was becoming a millionaire by providing accounting and consulting services to new companies that were struggling to survive. Coggins used his perceived talents to convince the entrepreneur, of these struggling companies to allow him to provide not only accounting services, but also manufacturing, business consulting services and investors. This is what helped inflate Matt's ego. He was a Certified Public Accountant (CPA), not an engineer, not a designer, not a rocket scientist, just a crooked CPA with lacking talents, but had "acquired" very rich acquaintances. He could convince desperate businessmen and women that he was capable of these services. He was extremely convincing. Matt

Coggins had all the qualities to serve as President of the United States for the current times. Coggins and Bill Clinton were definitely from the same mold. A mold that if destroyed, the world would and could only become a better place. With the lack of talents, he was just good at stealing, lying and manipulating the white collar way. Coggins didn't come cheap. In fact, he over billed a handsome rate and for everything, absolutely everything. He never understood, or let himself understand, the real reason the bait was always taken by these new companies, these young dreamers. He constantly convinced himself it was because he was "Matt Coggins—the everyone wants to be like me," ego. What he did understand was how to exploit the character of an entrepreneur. All entrepreneurs had a common attribute, all were ambitious and all were dreamers. They had dreams and visions that were barely attainable due to extreme obstacles. Most were extremely desperate after months that had turned into years of very hard, laborious work. Their only thought was to get some relief and assure a way to succeed. The workload was tremendous with back aching schedules. Days without ends, with minutes after minutes, hours after hours, all running together and being totally oblivious to issues other than accomplishing the needed deadlines. They did anything and everything that was needed to survive. Theft of a takeover was taught over and over and to such a great depth by all successful and maybe even more so by the unsuccessful entrepreneurs, especially theft by large corporations, but this concept was nowhere near the forefront of the entrepreneurs' minds. The thought of some big corporation stealing their ideas, was in the back of the mind, overlooking the fact it didn't necessarily have to be a large corporation, but even a small coquettish decorated CPA firm, could steal it. A road map was needed to find these fears through all the hopes and dreams that kept this optimistic few alive. Succeeding was all that mattered to these intelligent and talented few. These few were the ones that made the world tick and progress. Failing wasn't an option.

Matt's true dream was to have the talent to create, and run a company from the infancy stage, but he knew deep down and better than anyone he couldn't do it. His wife would often reiterate Matt's dream, to own a start up company. Something he could put his conniving hands on and carry through to the end. Incompetence, greed, lack of ethics and lack of intelligence in appropriate areas stood in his way. The only way he was going to get these companies was to use his power to steal. Stealing a dream was acceptable to him, after all it got him what he wanted and that was all he was interested in. The fact that he collaborated with Peters reinforced his ability to acquire his dream. Their flawed character did in fact make them good "white collar criminals." Coggins suffered from bi-polar disorder with some psychological tendencies, and this was the character flaw that actually acted as a catalyst in promoting his ambitions. He was good at using his ailment and unless one knew him well, most didn't know of his medical problems. When he was in his manic phase, which was most of the time, his "visions of grandeur" and high energy kept him going. It allowed him to put enormous amounts of needed energy and long hours into his acquisitions, so much so, in fact, he would go until he physically dropped. Once to this point, he would be forced to back off until the cycle repeated itself. He refused to take his medications when he was in his manic phase. This *was* his "talent" phase.

Matt and Derrik had a long history together. They were proud of one of the companies they had acquired in the past and it was a story they shared and bragged about upon numerous occasions. Their egos allowed them to tell anyone the story of Sal Lapero. Most people with this kind of story would have never mentioned it again, but to these two it was something they were both proud of. They would get a Santa Clause chuckle out of the story every time it was told. It was one of those stories that when the two of them would be laughing extremely hard, others listening would grin out of confusion, guessing they would have had to been there to get the gist of it. They could shoot the shit over that story for hours. These two were inadequate enough, that this Lapero story was the closest either of them got to the pleasure of a great sexual encounter. Accomplished criminals, malignant humans and greed mongrels were truly what were hidden behind these two facades that appeared as regular white collar, acceptable CPA's. Derrik allegedly helped frame Sal Lapero on an embezzlement charge that Matt and Derrik had allegedly schemed. It had never been proven, but all the facts pointed to these two. Insufficient proof was all there was at the time of the embezzlement. Charges were mentioned for obstruction of justice for destroying tons of Marquee Financial documents, but none of the charges ever stuck. Sal Lapero, Vice President of Marquee Financial was indicted on embezzlement charges two years earlier. Sal Lapero received all of his accounting services from Coggins and Coggins CPA firm. Susan Coggins participated in this venture and allegedly filed false tax returns. This venture had been under investigation by the IRS, but, to date, nothing could be pinned on the firm. Susan skirted along a fine line between legal and illegal many times in her accounting practices. She and the firm were always a few steps ahead of the IRS. Derrik had served as Chief Financial Officer to Marquee Financial and contracted Coggins for all accounting services. Lapero was arrested, with an attempt to show Coggins involvement. He pleaded guilty to conspiracy to commit wire fraud and money laundering. He also acknowledged the funneling of millions of dollars to Coggins through a myriad of financial schemes and agreed to cooperate with the investigation in return of a lighter sentence. Large sums of money had indeed been funneled through different accounts, but before Coggins could be implicated in the embezzlement, Coggins used his influence over some of the legal team with prior information he had on *them* on accounting issues he had provided to them over the years. Somehow, with enough conversations between Coggins and members of his legal team, the innuendos and charges connected with Sal Lapero were detoured. The detour was enough to let Coggins and Peters move on, but the cloud of the issue hung over them. There were nights Derrik had explained that he laid awake and worried about his house being bombed or he and his family getting blown away. Oddly enough, this is the part of the story that made him chuckle. He had a knack for inappropriate timing on laughter. The embezzlement at Marquee Financial had been a carefully flow-charted plan.

SOFT AND FLUFFY

Two days before Christmas, but only one day before Christmas Eve, the snow was falling in sheets of lacy white. *What could be better than this?* Jory thought. The trees were metamorphorizing into a whole new beauty. Jory was as excited as a child with a shiny new bike. From the time she moved to Texas she found herself slightly offended Texas didn't offer seasons in the style of the Midwest. Not having snow at Christmas was as unnatural as the "Ken doll" not having any genitals. Jory needed weather. Weather was symbolic. It offered changes, beauty, and it was extremely refreshing. It was all she needed to be reminded of the beauty and power of nature.

This was the Christmas Mason and Jory had waited for, for eight long years. Everything seemed so right, but there were millions of details to take care of before Christmas Eve and it was rapidly approaching. Christmas to Mason and Jory was a special time. Both looked forward to it with a child's anticipation. Both had surprises up their sleeves that would fill an extra large Christmas stocking. Perhaps even capable of filling Mason's five-foot, red and white, candy cane-striped, Christmas stocking. Since everything was bigger in Texas, Mason felt this should apply to his Christmas stocking in the same manner. Mason's Christmas present from Jory was almost too much for her to keep a surprise. Excitement and evaporation of the secret left Jory's mind and entered her mouth on several occasions, but fortunately the words stopped before any noise left her mouth. Tradition had it that each of their Christmas' had to have a theme. The theme for this Christmas was, "Soft and Fluffy." Only two more days—both could surely wait. Upon numerous occasions, telepathic messages had been exchanged between these two or so it goes, especially in the gift category. It was extremely difficult to surprise each other. These two were so intertwined that laughter entered many of their conversations when one would finish the sentence the other one had started. This was amusing until it came to presents and the surprises ended up not being surprises, more times than not. Jory was sure this would not be the case this year—or so she hoped.

Jory was to pick up the darling, actually "adorable" didn't even quite describe the rollie pollie puppy, Christmas Eve day. Jory was surprising Mason with a seven-week-old golden fluff ball known as a Golden Retriever puppy. Mason had a love for animals as pets and yet a manly urge to use them to assist him in hunting. What better gift to satisfy both, and of course, it also covered the years Christmas theme, not to mention satisfying Jory's love for animals. Jory had a special love for animals and truly believed animals were a gift. She had pets all of her life and was awed by their goodness. The love and forgiveness her pet dogs displayed was often more godly than the love and forgiveness of the human behavior.

Jory had already picked out their perfect dog from a litter of eight. She really wanted all eight, but she knew that wasn't quite sane. Even though she knew she had picked the perfect pup, that particular puppy would roll around and around and get mixed in with the seven others. When all of them were laying on their backs to get their fluffy tummies rubbed, the chosen one would disappear in the gold fluff, but two out of three times she was sure she kept picking the same one—pretty sure.

Oh, the excitement of this was just too much. Like a volcano about to erupt, her secret wanted to spew out in the same manner, but she could not—would not—spoil the surprise, not this close to Christmas.

It was about two in the afternoon and each snowflake was racing one after another from the sky as if running an Olympic race. Mason and Jory decided to go get their Christmas tree. It was past time, but this was the soonest they could get it done. At any rate, it was definitely their time. Mason remembered that as students, they could never afford much of a tree. Still not being much different financially, with the exception of their careers on the horizon and credit available, a bigger tree was more than a dream. It was a real possibility. He remembered the Longs Park Optimist Christmas tree lot. He and Jory used to admire those trees, but could never indulge. He drove them straight to Long's Park. Jory looked at him with such excitement and very quietly mumbled, "Oh, the Optimist trees, the prettiest trees." Mason had a warm, content feeling. He grabbed Jory's hand and they hurriedly went through the gate to the many isles of trees. There were several kinds, a million shapes and sizes, but only one smell, that fresh familiar piney, Christmas tree smell that couldn't help but make even the stalest heart—dance.

This was definitely a part of the Christmas spirit. How could it be that Scrooges ever existed? This was such a peaceful beautiful time of year to see God's work in everything. From the perfect pure white snowflakes, to the hustle and bustle of people shopping, the aroma from those beautiful trees awaiting a home and most of all the goodness of everything peaking from all corners of the earth. Yeh, maybe one would have to look, but without a doubt this time of year had goodness. Jory quickly had a thought of that fluffy little puppy and all of its goodness that was just waiting to be shared with Mason. She quietly jumped thoughts and shouted, "Oh, Mase, over there, look at that one."

Mason followed her in every snow-packed footprint she had left behind. As they approached and grabbed the seven-foot Douglas fir, Jory practically pushed Mason into the tree to *try* it.

"Oh, Mase, this is the one. Have you ever seen such a gorgeous tree?" Mason had already peeked at the price of the tree, but had no intention of bursting Jory's bubble over the price.

Mason hurriedly told Jory, "Merry Christmas, Jory—this tree was made for you, for us."

Jory was still bossing Mason around with the twirling of the tree to make sure every needle was in its given place.

A jolly, plump, white-haired little man had now entered the isle where Mason was holding up the tree. Only the red of Mason's coat could be seen through the dense tree to know someone was standing behind it. Telepathically, Mason and Jory shared the thought of how ironic it was to have a Santa Claus figure selling Christmas trees. Was it planned or a coincidence?

Clyde Schneiderman, a jolly, plump white haired little man came over to assist. "Ah, see ya fund the purfekt one!"

Mason answered, "This is it, this is the one." Jory was still bossing Mason to twirl the tree around and around to make sure every needle was still in its place. Jory was a little too symmetrical sometimes, and bossy—most times.

After joyfully purchasing the perfect tree, the two of them joined in the busy sidewalk of Christmas shoppers and stumbled on to a warm, cozy little coffee shop, Espresso Royale. Both had acquired a real taste for coffee these days. Mason with his regular cup of coffee added an extra shot of Espresso. His drink was often compared to a fine acid slurry that when a spoon was used to stir the drink the only thing left was a stub of the spoon or it was so strong it could support nails. Jory often threatened Mason she would hook up an IV coffee line to the side of the bed every morning for his little fix of caffeine. Jory's favorite drink was a "Café Con Leche," a mixture of milk with a small amount of coffee (she liked a little coffee with her milk). Of course it was just the opposite of Mason as so many qualities of the two were, but it was an opposition that provided continuity. Mason referred to her as a "rookie," lightweight, coffee drinker.

The day had been perfect. The anticipation of Christmas was beginning to peak. As the two sat in the coffee shop, piano music was dancing in the background with the warm, rich aroma of freshly brewed coffee hovering over the small café. The day was becoming more and more white, soft, pure white. The falling of the snow was mesmerizing, creating a peaceful trance. The warm feeling they were feeling in the pit of their stomachs was attributed to a combination of coffee and the season. Such contentment. It was getting late, dark and the snow was getting deep. It was almost deep enough to satisfy even Jory's insatiable need for deep snow. It was almost five in the afternoon and with winter expressing its presence, shopping was coming to a close. The two left reversing their earlier route. As they drove past Long Park, Mason noticed a jolly old man walking down the street holding hands with a jolly old woman. It was Mr. and Mrs. Schneiderman.

Mason looked at Jory and said, "Us in fifty years?"

She just smiled and knew exactly what he meant, but replied, "The plump part or the love part?"

"Both!" Mason answered, chuckling.

The snow was about six inches deep by early evening. The wind was howling from the north, arctic air was spiraling down. Mason trimmed and manipulated the fit of the tree into the snug green stand while Jory made a home for it. By midnight, the fireplace was crackling with warmth, radiating the whole house. The tree was decorated. It sparkled, and twinkled with vivid reds, greens and shimmers of silver. It was really a gorgeous tree and was relaxing to the human eye. Contentment sat in through the eyes of the soul. The two sat mesmerized by all the warmth and beauty and listened to the howling of the wind through the chimney. They warmed their hearts by the beauty and their bodies by the fire.

Mason and Jory decided to go upstairs to bed—Jory first, and then Mason following. Jory was going to surprise Mason with a "pre-Christmas" gift. It was a box of cracker jacks with the prize padded a little with the Star Wars figurine, "Jar Jar." Mason loved everything about the Star Wars episodes. This was just a little added extra gift. She loved doing this sort of thing, although, she was always disappointed on her capabilities to be creative. She finished getting ready for bed, tiptoed down the stairs, turned on a dim light and much to her surprise Mason had beaten her with his surprise for her. He had the same, exact idea. She gasped and was frozen in time for at least a second or two. She wasn't sure if it was from the cuddly teddy bear sitting in a big red sled smiling back at her or because she had ruined his surprise. She was giggling under her breath. She quickly placed the cracker jacks box with a big red bow under the tree and ran upstairs and hurriedly crawled into bed. Mason was close to sleep and unaware of her mischievous activities. Jory snuggled up against Mason as close as she could. The fraction of space between them was so small she was sure there wasn't an actual measurement for it. She noticed Mason's big sigh. Jory's hand started rubbing Mason's belly, eventually sliding her hand down further and further gently grabbing him. She felt him noticing. Jory had raised herself up to sit on top of him. She raised her tight, soft camisole over her head and let it fall to the floor. Mason reached up and felt her breasts, as he always did, as she worked herself on him. They made love until both were exhausted. Mason on his back then put his strong arm behind her and held her close.

Contentment of the evening continued. After a few minutes of enjoying their special time and winding down Jory let her mind wander until she felt sleepy. Jory had visions, not of sugar plums dancing through her mind, but of that big, soft snugly teddy bear downstairs, waiting for her. She pondered, *Now, was it acceptable to be thirty-two and still have a love for teddy bears? Probably not!* But it didn't stop her, she couldn't make the feeling stop, nor did she want to. She lay there coherent for a few minutes, trying to stay awake to make sure she wasn't missing anything. Falling asleep, she would miss watching Mason sleep and wondering what he was dreaming. Her dreams of him were sweet, so sweet, but they could never compare to the real thing. She loved to lie there and feel Mason's heart beat and see him breathing. Numerous times before falling asleep she wanted to capture the moment to stay with him in those private, precious moments. Her eyes were heavy, experiencing their final winking for the day, but simultaneously she thanked God for her wonderful life before she drifted into a deep, restful sleep.

SURPRISE ALLOWED

Finally, Christmas Eve arrived. Jory hurriedly got up and made an excuse that she forgot something she had to do. She told Mason she had to run to the store. Her mind was constantly racing as she pretty much babbled all morning about this and that to make the morning seem normal. Her babbling actually made it seem pretty abnormal. Her racing thoughts of getting that puppy and surprising Mason were consuming her mind. How was she going to do all this? She momentarily forgot about the surprises downstairs as she ran down the stairs as fast as she could. When she got downstairs she was surprised again and ran back upstairs as fast as she could. She went and jumped on Mason and wanted to share the excitement with him. In all the running up and down the stairs she managed to grab the teddy bear. She took her new soft friend and ran it across Mason's bare chest to wake him up.

He smiled. "I guess you've been into your presents? Just a little something until your main gift."

Jory had the teddy bear kiss Mason all over. "Merry Christmas, Merry Christmas, Merry Christmas," she repeated in a gruff voice for the bear as the bear pretended to kiss Mason. "Hurry you have to get up, too! Come downstairs with me."

Mason didn't ever rush in the mornings until he had several cups of coffee and a few hours behind him. He shuffled down the stairs and, too, was pleasantly surprised with *Jar Jar*.

Jory had to get on the road to Flush, Kansas, fifteen minutes east of Manhattan. There was a new family member impatiently waiting.

The plan was to have Mason stay behind; after all it was just an errand. Jory got into the Trooper, contemplating the fifteen degree slope of her snowy driveway. It was definitely a four-wheel drive morning. The snow had stopped falling, but it was at least six to eight inches deep. The sun peaked around a cloud, timidly lighting up the morning. She got about five minutes away and stopped. "No, this would be better with Mason," she mumbled. Everything always was. She turned the Trooper around and hurried back home to pick up Mason. What story was she going to make up to get him to go with her? Mumbling, Jory quietly spoke, "Man, now what am I going to tell him?"

"Mase, Mase, quick, you have to come with me. I want to show you something!" She took the palm of her hand and smacked it against her forehead and quietly said, "Now that was real original!"

Of course, Mason being the engineer he was, had to know all the facts.

"It's a surprise, just come with me, please, please, please." Again, she couldn't believe this was as creative as she got. Creativity, proven once again, definitely wasn't one of her strong points. All this time, she had been quiet about the surprise and now she blatantly told him she had a surprise. This was so tedious for her. "Oh, Mase, just come with me, okay? I'll buy you a cup of coffee."

She knew this coercion technique would work. "Yeah, coffee, that's it." This was all it took? She couldn't believe how inversely proportional her anxiety was to Mason's fix for coffee. "Coffee was the answer, unbelievable," she mumbled.

Back to the little café, for opposite coffees and then they were on their way to get that new member of the family.

SOCKS AND PARKING PLACES

As when Jory first picked out the puppy, a gold ball of fur rolling around on the powder white grass was all that could be seen when they arrived at the farmhouse where the Golden Retrievers awaited their new family. The only difference today was the puppy had snow all over its black button nose and a red bow tied around his furry neck. Mason just laughed when he saw what was transpiring. That laugh came from his heart and through his beautiful green eyes. When Mason sincerely smiled, his eyes smiled. "Merry Soft and Fluffy Christmas," Jory said as she hugged Mason and the new puppy.

The shivering puppy looked as if it was freezing to death. It was so frightened of these new strangers. After all, these two that had just taken him from his family. Unaware, he was just about to have the best life any dog could hope for.

Mason held and consoled the fluffy puppy all the way back home. He took his warm hands and stroked the puppy's soft head. Sam, Jake, Chiowaka, Hank, Spanky were just a few of the names thrown out for discussion. This was such an important decision; after all, it was a new member of the family. After about one hundred names, Mason blurted out the perfect name, "Hobbes!" Jory had often referred to the similarities of the comic *Calvin and Hobbs* to Mason. Mason's character was Calvin and now a Hobbes. Hobbes it was.

So the Christmas of 1998 came and went. It was one of the more perfect ones either of them could remember. Mason, Jory and Hobbes all riding the sled through the powdered snow at their neighborhood park, roast duck for Christmas dinner, abundant presents, a family gathering with their, what Jory referred to as the "cozillion", Kansas relatives. Overall, it was a warm, beautiful holiday. The peacefulness and gratitude of the season had carried them through to a new beginning. The beginning they had worked on their entire life together. They had made it with a home, a family and a life. And a great life it was.

TRANSITIONS

Several pleasant months had passed. Hobbes had become a big part of the family. The dog could carry on a conversation as well as any person, without ever saying a word. Hobbes went absolutely everywhere with Mason and Jory. He heard, saw and did all they did. He was indeed becoming a best friend to both, and a "guardian angel" to Jory. Hobbes had a big vocabulary for a dog. Jory talked to him *all* the time. She talked to him about everything from general conversations to being her audience as she would prepare for a professional lecture. Jory had a habit of making up songs to correspond with what was going on for the day. She was an adult and she was still singing to her dogs just like she did on those warm summer days back on her farm. One day when she finished her new lyrics she added "everybody now" in which Mason chimed in and then Hobbes started howling. Hobbes was not going to be left out of anything. There was an unspoken understanding. Hobbes was definitely a little person disguised as a dog. He heard it all. His ears responded accordingly. Up and down like a puppet when one of the recognizable words were mentioned. He was a very good, obedient dog. Hobbes had learned to be a soft furry friend to everyone. He had many roles. Friendship, protector, playmate and just plain ole companionship. There was no other dog like him. In the neighborhood, Gray's home was known as Hobbes' home. He didn't have a mean bone in his body. He kept watch for all the kids and kept an eye on his, Mason and Jory's territory. He routinely went outside and secured the perimeter before going inside for the night. Mason as well as Jory had spent hours training and disciplining Hobbes. As time went on, there was an affirmation that animals were happier when there was an understanding of obedience. It was obvious that Hobbes would have the wisdom of what was important in life, in his short life, one could only hope acquiring in a long lifetime.

Mason had been through several of the aching steps of an entrepreneur. In the infancy stage it was a real struggle to raise funds. After six months, several paths had been explored. Mason first went to individuals with some, but limited success. Mason had figured to really get this company going he would need at a minimum, two hundred and fifty to five hundred thousand dollars. With family, friends and private investors, he had raised about fifteen thousand. His first real step would have to be to incorporate the company. Mason had received a name of an attorney in Topeka, Kansas, that could incorporate the new company. The first stone turned over would lead Mason and Jory entering a plush office with the name "Owen, Curtis and Watson." They entered the tenth floor, panoramic view office of Jim Watson. A tall, distinguished bald gentleman appeared. At first glance, "gentleman" was a very fitting term. It then became obvious that this man must be making some grandchild very happy being a perfect grandpa. Mason explained why he was there and that he needed to incorporate a new company. Of course he started with the fact that he was a mechanical engineer with a new idea. He proceeded to explain how Jory had this idea to automate pharmacies. Mason explained that his idea would be to have a shelf like unit that would hold two hundred drugs, a robotic arm, four vial containers and an interface that would connect to existing pharmacy computers. Mason described this whole process like it was old hat, when in fact it had never been done. With such a need, it seemed someone would have thought of it. Whenever Mason would talk about engineering so "matter of factly" he would generally lose his audience to "mind drifting" because most couldn't understand his level of intelligence on such matters. All through the explanation of his system Mason kept noticing there wasn't any expression from this man as he quietly chewed and chewed his Nicorette gum, obviously acquiring a new habit, chewing—not smoking or perhaps both. In fact, during Mason's technical explanations of his system, Mr. Watson felt an interruption and an explanation was necessary for this new habit. "I'm trying to quit smoking" he said with a faint hint of a smile, "please continue." After about thirty minutes of actual technical information—the "invented" facts had been told and nervousness took over Mason's body. This was a natural response to Mr. Watson's expressionless demeanor. Feeling like he had just described a brilliant idea, Mr. Watson, with an inquisitive look on his smooth face, swallowing all of the juice from his nicotine gum finally spoke. "Mr. Gray, I can't help you!" Mason's heart dropped.

In his mind, Mason thought, *Great, I must have spent an hour describing my idea and all I am going to get is a whopping bill from this guy!* Mason had to admit he did have a negative, stereotypical attitude about attorneys. After all what other profession could charge exorbitant amounts? He only knew of one other profession, the oldest, that paralleled this line of thinking and charging, but it wasn't legal.

Jolted from his thoughts, Mason heard, "No, Mr. Gray, I am going to send you across the street to a buddy of mine. Goodwell, Edwards, Smith and Behrens will be a better firm for you. With your permission, I have several buddies I would like to approach about investing in your company. Mr. Gray, I believe you may have re-invented the mouse trap!"

Mason couldn't believe his ears. Jory was elated and was struggling to contain herself. She wanted to adopt this man as her grandpa and give him a big hug, but she showed restraint and stayed professional.

Her eyes brightened like a new morning sun that had accomplished the journey up and over the horizon.

Mason and Jory wanted to jump up and down like two small children who just entered an amusement park, but both of them kept their composure and professionalism as long as necessary. This was truly a "Godsend." Mr. Watson did have three other elderly friends that invested another fifteen thousand dollars to start Dispensing Innovations (DI) and allowed the company to incorporate. In exchange for their money they truly just wanted stock in the company. A fair deal it was. Mr. Watson did indeed send Mason and Jory across the street to meet with another attorney named Bill Edwards. This man was supposed to be the head guru of securities. When this attorney entered the room Mason and Jory subconsciously thought about the age of all these individuals and that their health could enter into the equation of the success of this venture. So far, all the gentlemen involved were over sixty-five years of age, and a few—way over. None of this was in the forefront of their minds and didn't seem to matter at this point in time. In fact, there was a comfort that their age and success possibly reflected money was no longer their main goal in life.

Bill Edwards was a jolly, large burly man (a Santa Clause figure). He immediately took Mason and Jory under his wings and guided them the best he could. He was stern but helpful. He became DI's corporate attorney, incorporating the company and setting it up as an "S" corporation. Step by step, detail by detail. Every day for the next three months there was contact between the three of them to finalize the legalities.

Mason left no stone unturned, ever. For the next few weeks, Mason was on the phone every day, all day long. Everything was happening incredibly fast. Doors opened. Doors closed. Doors opened. Doors closed. More closed than opened, but at least some opened. Mason never lost hope. Never. He knew to be a success, giving up or failing was not an option. Ever. His entrepreneurial excitement was contagious. He would do this. And he *could* do this.

Gray's house became their place of business. Up to now, any

concept testing was done in the garage. The garage, the bedrooms, the solarium, all rooms were recruited and occupied with the automated dispensing system (ADS) parts.

It was three o'clock in the afternoon, September 1999 when the doorbell rang. Mason accepted a certified letter from the mailman. The gray letter was from the Technology Enterprise Corporation (TEC). TEC provided grants from state lottery money, to new companies for their inventions. There wasn't a lot of money to be given making the selection of awards limited. Mason had applied for a grant for his system that would allow him the cash to build the first prototype system and use Kansas State University, their students and staff as employees. Since so many doors closed every day, Mason was hopeful but realistic. He opened the letter and he felt his heart skip several beats. The letter read, "Congratulations!" Mason barely needed to read any further, but, at the same time, he couldn't read fast enough and scanned the letter for the big information. Twenty thousand dollars stood out in bold letters. Mason had been granted the twenty thousand to get this idea started. What a great start. He realized this was not even close to enough money, but it was still a great start. Someone believed in him. Disregarding the money, someone took him serious and saw the potential. Victory number one! The yahoos and the jump-roping jumps had filled the house. Mason liked to refer to this as the engineering, "happy dance." Somewhere and somehow this was a commonality between his engineering friends that only that specific group understood. Engineers didn't usually come wired with a lot of expressions. Mason was definitely an exception.

M&M's

It was a sunless, snowy day in March. Patents had been applied for. Mason already had patents from companies he had worked for in the past, but this was a first for Jory. Needless to say she took the excitement from it to the extreme. She literally glowed from knowing it was her idea. From this point on, whether the company was successful or not, she changed the profession of pharmacy, forever. It was a real moral booster. She was doing all of the market studies. She felt compelled to be the one to call on her fellow pharmacists and ask a set of specific questions to see exactly how accepted this whole idea of pharmacy automation would be. After one hundred calls and many hours of visiting, she proved that other pharmacists felt the same about the whole subject. More time was indeed needed for pharmacists to do what they were trained to do—freeing them from the repetitive, mundane tasks like counting and pouring. They wanted more time to visit with their patients and educate them on the proper use of their medication. They were willing to pay for any technology that would allow them this opportunity. It was a win-win situation for all.

"HELLO, we need a name, a good successful name!" Jory exclaimed.

The naming of the company had been fun and exciting. After hours of serious names, crazy ones were thrown in every once in a while when everyone was punchy, but eventually Dispensing Innovations, Inc., won the title. Along with the process, the machine initially would be known as the Automated Dispensing System (ADS). There, it was settled and this process seemed to make it official. ADS was the name of the prototype, but as improvements were made and the machine took on perfection it was licensed under the name RxBot the automated dispensing system. The trademark was now owned by Dispensing Innovations, Inc.

Mason and Jory took every textbook precaution to protect their invention. Incorporate (but ALWAYS keep control), insure, insure, insure, apply for patents, keep an updated business plan, have really good "ethical" attorneys, both realizing "ethical attorneys" may be an oxymoron. They did the whole gamut. The two went by the book and did it all. Funds were very limited, but priorities were priorities—and they kept them.

Production of the prototype was coming together fairly smoothly. Even stumbling blocks were not unpleasant. Mason was as happy as a lark. If something didn't work properly, well all the better. After all, he was born to invent and fix anything broken. Mason had a philosophy that one needed to enjoy the process no matter where it might lead. This was an extremely important concept to him.

Day after day, parts and pieces were converging to conform. Mason sincerely believed "necessity is the mother of invention." A new genesis. This system was a piece of art. Communicating in its own way. Tweaking became the word of the season. Every waking moment was spent at Kansas State University in the basement of Durland Hall. Room 21 and 22 became Mason's second home. Lunches and dinners were brought in. Meetings were often scheduled for all members of the design team to demonstrate the latest version of their creation and their areas of design. There were meetings for budgetary purposes and progress purposes. Meetings,

meetings, meetings. Hot, gooey, chocolate brownies were known to show up at one o'clock in the morning and were very much welcomed. It was a very busy time, but a very pleasant atmosphere. Progressive, persistent and pleasant.

The early spring brought open house to Kansas State University. Open house was an annual event for the university that brought in thousands of people. One part of the machine called the "cell" made a fascinating engineering "show and tell." The part looked simple, but demanded the largest amount of time and money to design. It was a true engineering challenge. This was one of the patented parts because it was unique and extremely necessary for a good design to the whole system. This part needed to be smooth, have the ability to align tablets and capsules to form a single line and make the capsules and tablets fall into a vial and then be counted as they dropped one after the other. Of course the cell design wasn't perfected, but Mason decided to show it at open house demonstrating with M&M's instead of tablets. It was a hit. Men, women, children, students and faculty all wanted a chance to get a vial of M&M's. One by one they would walk up to the device, grab a paper cup and hold it under the cell in front of the sensor to activate the spinning action. This would line the M&M's up for departure into the vial. The only step that wasn't automated was the ole hand to mouth movement. One fascinating point, to Mason, was the fact that the engineering faculty members were the only individuals that tried to avoid the technology by walking up and grabbing a cup and dipping it in the top of the "cell" rather than letting the device do its thing. Mason found this ironic since these were the individuals teaching the technology. Many academics were notorious for "standing still in time" in their teachings.

Within a few weeks the prototype would be complete. July 1, was the scheduled completion day. Then what? Back to square one. Out of money. Again. Mason, trying to spend every moment on building the machine still had to constantly work on raising funds. Mason always remained optimistic. All the market studies indicated this was something pharmacists wanted and needed. All indicators were a go!

The first few months were like being on a roller coaster. When the adrenaline was at an all time high that "ole" roller coaster's momentum would just about expire upon reaching the apex, only to begin a rapid descent. The rush of the ride was needed to keep the energy going. It was an incredibly exciting, invigorating few months. The dream was coming to life and everyone involved was enjoying the process.

As the July scheduled completion date approached, money was disappearing extremely fast. Mason knew he had to spend some more time on getting more money injected into this project to keep it viable. The machine would be moving back to their home soon. Jory was filling her time at the pharmacy and any spare time she could rustle up she lent a hand to the creation too. There was talk and dreams that if all went well she would have to devote full-time to DII.

One Saturday morning in May, Mason jumped out of bed and told Jory, "This is the day I go out and get money. I won't be back until I sell a machine!" As she fidgeted and smiled nervously she added her optimism and respect for Mason to do this. In the back of her mind, she was reluctant to the idea that she may not see Mason for quite some time if he was serious about not returning until he sold a machine, but, on the other hand, there was also a possibility he would return after the meeting with the first client.

Over the months, names had been given to either Mason or Jory of "so and so" who knew of "somebody" else who MAY be interested in either the company or the machine or both. The list grew and grew for POTENTIAL investors which naturally led to a lengthy list of people NOT interested, but it would only take a few to get the ball rolling. At this point, everyone was a potential investor. If they had a dime to spare and showed any interest what's so ever, then they would be contacted.

One name in particular Mason kept coming upon was John Crowe. He was a pharmacist in Salina, Kansas. Jory got his name at the pharmacy and he was known as a real "go-getter." He loved to get involved in new "things" and he had lots of money. Better yet, he was a "sure thing." He was an all around trusted pharmacist. Obviously, he had to be one of the participants of the gallop poll pharmacists are always talking about. That poll often ranks pharmacists at the top as being the, "most respected profession."

Mason pulled up slowly to the Miller Clinic in Salina that housed John Crowe's pharmacy. As he approached the entrance, he was surprised at how small the pharmacy actually was. He could tell that physical size must not be an issue for this little "gold mine" since every patient that came to this clinic stopped and visited the pharmacy on their way out. It was definitely a product of design by John Crowe. This pharmacy was small, but it had all the right ingredients. Of course, it met all the medical necessities, but it had a fun loving yet professional staff that offered that much-needed tender loving care.

Mason was now peering in the large pane windows, pausing for a moment to watch all the activity inside. It was like one of those mechanical music boxes where there's movement everywhere. He felt a warm feeling as he watched a middle age man in a blue smock set down with a gray-haired, feeble, elderly woman. He pointed to directions on the label of the prescription vial and opened the non-child-proof lid to show the worried woman that the tablets were small enough for her to swallow. Mason thought, *Now that's service, but how in the world does he find the time?* People were lined up to the back of the pharmacy and out into the clinic hallway. They were everywhere and there wasn't even an "everywhere" to this pharmacy.

This stone, when turned over had a prize under it.

With the TEC awarded grant, continuous interest followed based on TEC's reputation alone. The award spawned interest from the Kansas Ways and Means Committee and the House Appropriations Committee. They wanted to view the machine. Mason and Jory were excited, but the only option they had was to bring these influential people to their modest two-car garage for the showing.

Jory explained to Mason, "This will be really embarrassing!" There were no funds, yet, to allow for a proper showing.

"This could be advantageous showing the commitment and the need for this company," Mason explained.

The State Legislatures visited the Gray's as part of a tour of state funded facilities. Jory sat up tables of refreshments as the legislatures toured through the spotless garage. It ended up being a very enjoyable visit, meeting very influential people as well as showing off their creation.

The local newspaper also ended up being there and wrote a story of the event. One of the quotes in the paper probably hit the closest to the truth at that point. "Dealing with new start up companies is extremely exciting, but it is also frustrating because you have to raise 'risk' money. Even if the Gray's could pull off getting more funds to meet their needs it would still be all on a 'shoestring budget,' creating a large risk!"

After Jory read the article she was elated, but there was a drop in her gut when she saw the truth printed about "shoestring budget." That wasn't anything new to her, but seeing it in writing somehow made her extremely uneasy.

SOLD

The meeting with John Crowe went surprisingly well. The gentleman turned out to be very enthusiastic. Word had already reached John about an ambitious young couple creating a machine that would automate a portion of pharmacy. After just one meeting, and covering every detail, John acted as if he was ready to buy a machine. Mason could tell he was dead serious about getting involved with DII and his need for a machine like he had invented. This was enough for Mason, today.

After an extremely, long memorable day, Mason arrived home still bursting with energy from the sale of his first machine. Opening the front door, blurting from his mouth, "Remember, I told you I wouldn't be back until I sold a machine? Well...I'm back!"

The following week John made a trip to Manhattan to view the creation of the automated machine. He expected a lot, but he was in total awe when confronted face to face with the birthing of this creation. He could barely contain his enthusiasm and after visiting only one day he wanted to order the first machine. At this point, Mason had figured he could sell the machine and make a nice profit if the selling price would be forty thousand dollars. This would be an attractive price for the targeted pharmacies. It was affordable and allowed most medium size pharmacies a two-year payback. Mason, too, could barely believe what he was hearing and his excitement was invigorating. John also wanted to make the deal a business/partnership. He wanted the first machine, but he also wanted some ownership in this new company. Mason was willing to work any kind of deal, with the one exception of keeping to the fast rule of keeping control of the company. He could tell John was someone that could be trusted and also had a heart for entrepreneurs. It didn't take long to get this deal packaged up. John Crowe placed the first order and also acquired ten percent ownership. Needless to say the twenty thousand dollar down payment helped tremendously and also created credibility that was very needed to get additional sales and funding. The company was still small and much expertise was still needed. John Crowe would serve as a Board of Director and offer his expertise in many, many areas.

JACK-OF-ALL-TRADES BUT MASTER OF NONE

After the uniting of Mason and John Crowe, a true path was unveiling its way. The prototype did meet deadlines and resulted in a completely amazing functioning "example" of a machine. John not only brought additional pharmacy expertise, but he brought financial support in himself and with his many friends. Over the next few months John helped gather people he knew that wanted to get involved and were willing to invest money. Venture capitalists, Board of Pharmacies, Pharmacy Associations and the like all were gathered to view and discuss directions of RxBot—The Automation for Pharmacy. People never ceased to be amazed after they viewed the machine as it whistled and danced its routine for the future of pharmacy. Jory was the one to demonstrate RxBot. She understood the issues of pharmacy and felt very proud and comfortable showing it off among her colleagues. She met face to face with the individuals of the State Board of Pharmacy to discuss the changes and additions to the laws that affected automation. They all made themselves comfortable at the large conference table exchanging ideas. Her eyes danced as she explained the whole concept. Her enthusiasm was contagious. Jory loved this professional opportunity and all of her new friends being involved in her idea. She had an influence on these people and she never had a clue to what extent.

After several months of showing RxBot and getting the first machine moved in to John Crowe's Pharmacy and working, RxBot became like an adopted child and was even given a name by the staff of John Crowe's pharmacy. They called it Einstein (Einy for short) and in time it was referred to only by *its* name. Many, many dollars had been spent. Money was constantly going to attorneys to maintain keeping everything "safe" and above board. After Mason orchestrated months of work on the technology, the investors and attorneys had put together a "Limited public offering" to raise two hundred and fifty thousand dollars to allow DII to sell and make five more machines. The Public Offering was a success and ongoing. It did bring in enough funds to allow the five machines to be made. In the mean time, interest continued to grow at an alarming rate. Mason and Jory saw the potential for this small company, but were becoming very familiar with the concept of growing to fast. It was a double-edged sword and a nice problem to have, too much interest, and not enough money or people, at this point. The company would have to evolve quickly to support the interest. Interest and the production had to be as equal as possible. This was an incredible hurdle to accomplish. Mason knew the interest problem was close to insurmountable and had wished numerous times he had invented some five cent item instead of something that cost thousands of dollars to make, but there was no turning back at this point and now it all depended on timing and a whole lot of luck. The stress levels were increasing and the roller coaster was at a gradual incline.

Mason and Jory wore all hats. One morning Jory was driving down the street and the cell phone started to ring. Jory used the cell phone for the company phone. "Dispensing Innovations, may I help you?" she answered.

"May I speak to Jory Gray?" the calming, intellectual voice asked.

Jory hated to admit she was the one answering the phone, but she had little choice.

She pulled herself together to confidently admit it was her speaking.

"This is Bill Thererr from Walgreen's and I have heard that you have an automated prescription dispensing machine."

Of course, Jory had to immediately pull over to the side of the road, not only to catch her breath, but also to compose herself. Now, more than ever, she needed to be professional in taking this call from the Chief Financial Officer of the largest pharmacy chain in the nation. The call was a success and Mr. Thererr had requested Mason and Jory to come to Chicago and visit with the Board of Directors of Walgreen's about the possibility of using their machine.

"Oh my God, this is unbelievable!" Jory blurted when she hung up the phone. The excitement was overwhelming. This was one of the most rewarding and worthwhile efforts she had done in her life. The small town pharmacist and engineer were meeting with the Board of Directors of a major chain, pharmacy. This alone was an enormous accomplishment and wherever the path would lead this would be a momentous occasion for the two of them. To be called by Walgreen's, driving down a city street by a Pizza Hut in the small little town of Manhattan, Kansas, represented so many issues on so many levels. Could they do this? Time would tell. Some major changes had to take place. A building had to be rented for the company. The business had to take on a more professional image. Money was limited, but it had come to a time where it had to move forward. There had to be a way to figure out how to do this. The two immediately went looking for a cheap, functional place to rent. Their excitement should have been worth something. They were so proud. In very little time, with such limited options, they found a place, a small two (and a half) room place. One room was manufacturing, the other an office. The half of room was a restroom. At least it was a place of business and it could be rented by the month. Until something further developed, this would have to do until moving to a bigger place could be accomplished. The two acted as the company accountants, marketing staff, sales force, engineers, pharmacists, purchasers, you name it, and they did it— or at least tried. How were they going to continue in this capacity? There wasn't money available to pay very many people to put on staff and the amount of energy it was taking from the both of them was draining. It was decided, by the company, that Mason would draw a small salary and Jory a part-time salary which left enough for a mediocre receptionist. The money had to buy a nice voice and enough intelligence to organize calls. It was a start. Jory, coaxed her brother, Mark into helping with sales. He lived in Los Angeles—but even better. Los Angeles was a huge market in itself. It didn't matter because technology made it possible to work together. In this day of modern technology, emails, faxes, cell phones and the like made the world so small. It was practically like they were in the same office. Mark was proud to become the "West Coast Sales Manager." He did an exceptional job, which could have been interpreted as bad news since it created more sales and interest, which in turn demanded more personnel. Jory again recruited more family, her brother Joe, who was a pilot. He offered his plane and sales expertise as much as possible, free at this point. Jory coaxed her friend and sister-in-law, Maddie to be the corporate accountant. She was such a good friend and one of the top accountants of all time. She was totally competent and trustworthy. She was more than happy to help and in just a short amount of time the company grew by three professional staff. With Mason and Jory, if there was a will there was a WAY.

Money, money, money and more money was needed. This was a constant job all in itself. Investors were welcomed, along with working on a limited public offering and an application for a Small Business Administration loan. If all went well this could actually work. Nothing happened quickly; after all, Rome wasn't built in a day as the ole saying goes.

It was a sunny afternoon when an elderly, friendly gentleman strolled into the one room office that DII was renting. He had heard through the grapevine about this company and was in the business of renting buildings. He had the perfect building for this small company.

His name was Walter Simms. Walter was persistent and convinced the young couple to at least look at what he had to offer. Coincidentally, this was how many things fell into place with this company. Now, why would Mason and Jory look at a building when they couldn't afford any staff? Stepping-stone after stepping-stone brought just enough money in to make that next step, very carefully. Walter was so convincing and gave them such a good deal and on top of that he wanted to invest in the company making it possible to rent the building. For rent he would gain some ownership in the company. He also had a brother that would be interested. The building was too large, but if growth continued at its current rate, it could be the perfect building. It was wide and open for manufacturing and had a few offices for the intended staff.

Struggling day to day, money kept trickling in and kept the company going. Progress continued. In November, one of the many calls of the day, requested to talk to Jory Gray. "Hello, this is Jory, May I help you?"

The voice on the other end was a woman with a professional voice, "Hello, I am Kim Eakins with "Pharmacy Topics."

"Pharmacy Topics" was one of the best pharmacy journals distributed nationally to pharmacist in all practices. Jory could barely contain herself. The editor proceeded to invite Jory to do an interview article about RxBot that would be released in the February issue. Jory ecstatically agreed to do the interview giving full names of her and Mason and all the background information. She proceeded to tell the story of that last, long lecture from the Veteran's Administration explaining the need of automation when she was in pharmacy school. Subconsciously, she was thinking how long ago that lecture seemed—a lifetime ago. She and Mason had discussed how to answer certain questions about the completion of the machine, sales and the company, honestly, but to make sure not too much information would be given on how small the company actually was at the time, to ensure being taken seriously. The fact that it was mainly the two of them would obviously create a warranted concern on how a company this small would be able to keep up. Jory explained to the editor that the current plan was that five machines were going to be sold and distributed by May, 2001. Sounding very professional and fortunately she was speaking to an editor verses a technical person, offered the opportunity to pull off that DII knew what they were doing and knew how they were going to be a success. The two honestly believed this was how it would be, but each step was not written in stone, yet. In a small company, like DII, nothing ever had time to be written in stone. Change was constant. After about thirty minutes, the first interview, for this newly formed company, on this first automated prescription machine, was over.

Jory hung up, literally jumped out of her chair yelling, "Holy Shit, Pharmacy Topics, WE ARE BIG TIME!" The roller coaster geared up with major momentum.

The phone rang again and again, but the last call of the day plunged the roller coaster into a descent. Bill Edwards was rushed to the hospital and it appeared he had a brain tumor. Bill had constantly been the guiding attorney for the company. His guidance was needed. He was a *unique*. He cared and had the intelligence to help this company and keep them from harms way. He allowed them to make payments as money was available which was of great importance at this point and highly unusual for an attorney. There were numerous times Bill was fascinated by this whole concept. He cheered them on in many ways. He did everything possible to help. This was not a commonality throughout the firm; in fact it was an oddity. Bill was such a good person on top of being exactly what the company needed in an attorney. The stones that were unturned to meet Bill completed a needed path. He was a friend and he wanted the Grays' to succeed. He was a mentor on the legalities.

This was extremely bad news in more than one way. Of course the possibility of losing a friend was the worst of it, but after several minutes on the phone with another partner of the firm, it was suggested to find a new attorney, at the same firm. Bill may not be back. His future looked very grim. Unknown at the time, it was probably suggested to stay with the firm because of the amount of money DII already owed and not out of concern for the clients.

SOCKS AND PARKING PLACES

A new attorney was assigned to the newly formed company. The loss of Bill Edwards as an attorney had many unfortunate consequences. Phil Kalivoda was one of them. He was going to be the new attorney. He couldn't have been any more opposite from Bill if he tried. His first gruff words to Mason were, "Now let's see, you owe our firm a substantial amount of money and I don't see how we can go forward until this money is paid in full." Mason tried to explain that Bill had worked out a deal for the company, but Phil quickly and rudely interrupted, "Bill, isn't your attorney any more! You can take it or leave it, but if you leave it you still owe us twelve thousand dollars and I will not help you until you pay ME in full."

Mason wondered if "ME" was a Freudian or did this jerk really think he deserved the money? Mason's heart dropped. He knew this was going to be another uphill battle. He thought to himself, *What's one more battle added to this whole scenario?* Proven right, every conversation with Phil started on billing issues with such little interest of the matters at hand. It was going to be a long haul on the legal aspects, as well.

PROGRESSION

Fast minutes turned into fast hours, fast hours into fast days, fast days into fast weeks, fast weeks to fast months, fast months to fast years, which appeared to be about as fast as the ole German saying, "Einen Augenblick", translated to mean, *in a blink of the eye*. Three very quick, *long* years had passed. Three years of multiple venture capitalist agreements ALMOST made, three years of small company mergers, ALMOST made, three years of big corporation takeovers or mergers, ALMOST made when in fact the only real financial influx was still from private individuals, the limited public offering and the Small Business Administration loan. It trickled in like an old dried up spring, but flowed out like a raging rapid. Many, many contacts were made which led to many, many more contacts. Financial concerns were ongoing, every day, all day long and in between all the other business aspects that needed to be taken care of. There was always enough frustration to go around, but limited success shadowed the company as well. It was limited, but it was there. The business deals were always close at hand, but rule number one kept interfering; "Don't ever relinquish control—EVER!"

There were companies with voice activation equipment that were interested. There were companies that made Kodak photography equipment that were interested. And then not to mention all the Joe Blows. Many "Joe's" had a lot of money and just wanted to pick up the company for complete control and had limited knowledge on the product or the industry it was to serve. The closest and ongoing deal that looked the most attractive was with Graham Pharmaceutical, one of the **biggest** pharmaceutical companies in nearly the entire world. They wanted to get involved with DII in some way and had all the right pieces to do it. Graham already had automation developed, but it was never quite state of the art. It was a clunkier type of automation system. It would be more attractive for warehouse automation rather than for a retail setting, but opportunity for both companies was apparent and an option. Of course, nothing could ever be done without the approval of the Board of Directors, but the company was small enough things could be decided pretty fast with limited involvement from the attorneys. Once the attorneys were involved time halted to a snails pace since they were paid by the hour. What a system. Throughout the history of this company, among all involved, it was a fear that a big corporation would come in and steal the idea and leave all of DII behind, high and dry.

The venture capitalist interest also continued to grow. These groups had to be responsible for the concept of "hoop jumping." They were obviously modified bankers with bigger, modified egos. After about one trillion meetings, it became clear that even if they were serious and interested, maybe especially if they were interested, then there were an infinite number of hoops one must jump through. Mason, along with the Board of Directors did a lot of jumping. The hoop jumping was expensive, time consuming, frustrating, but still unexpectedly provided hope. Hope was a very important component that needed to be sustained. The experience obtained through this whole financial fiasco was not something that was ever taught in management classes in college or in any other class for that matter. This was definitely the school of hard knocks. Some knocks were so hard that everyone involved found themselves picking themselves up and dusting off the ole britches and starting all over again.

While all of the financial meandering took place, business ran on a day-to-day routine. Marketing and sales continued, demonstrations were made, and closing contracts continued. Local interest sprouted from demonstrations at the Country Club to radio station interviews and all the local newspapers with some of the following headlines reading, KANSAS WINNERS, COUPLE CREATE TIME SAVING PILL DISPENSING MACHINE, MANHATTAN COUPLE/ PHARMACY MACHINE AUTOMATES PHARMACY, university papers headlining, ALUMNI AND HUSBAND PATENT PHARMACY AUTOMATION, and numerous presentations to student groups, entrepreneur groups and anyone that wanted to know about RxBot. Jory was incredibly proud that all the reputable pharmacy journals had now contacted her and wanted to write articles about her and Mason and their invention. Pictures were displayed, quotes were printed and interest spread like wildfire about this small, determined company and their product. DII had now changed dispensing in pharmacies, forever. DII did meet the deadline for the five machines and had made contracts to pharmacies that had agreed to be beta test sites. This proved to be a win-win situation for everyone. Pharmacies got a great product for a great price with the understanding that improvements were still needed. After three years, this was working well, but money was desperately limited and something needed to happen fast. DII again received five more orders to deliver RxBot machines over the next nine months. Whether it could be done remained to be seen. National, local and individual interest had made this company real. It was a kinetic company, charged, but still with meager means.

    Mason and Jory worked extremely hard. Crawling across the Sahara desert might have been equated to this experience. They became true business partners and complimented each other's expertise with knowing where the line was and where it was NOT all right to cross. Unfortunately, there wasn't much time for anything else. They were traveling to the east coast, traveling to the west coast and everywhere in between. International interest was starting. Even

SOCKS AND PARKING PLACES

Saudi Arabia, Hong Kong and Japan wanted either a company representative to come to their site or send a DVD or download online media of this automated pharmacy system.

Because of the funding and expenses, marketing had to be creative and cheap. Surprisingly the combination could be done. Friends were hired to do a marketing DVD. A husband and wife duo that had a small media company out of their home decided to do the DVD for exchange of stock. The relationship worked out well both in business and as well as the four became good friends. They did an excellent job and once again it was hard to keep up on the supply of DVD's. Jory would review the Wall Street Journal daily to give her ideas. She often thought, *Hey, why not learn from the best?* When the Wall Street Journal used full-page ads, Jory would reverse that idea of marketing. She thought, *Why not small, like postcards?* That's exactly what she did. She used catchy phrases like, "RXBOT INTRODUCES PROFITS!" and then lots of small print in between. It worked well. They were cheaper to send and print. After they were printed, they were sent to all pharmacies within the target market.

While Jory was doing all the marketing, Mason continued to struggle in keeping the designs simple. Jory insisted that there could not be any adjustments for pharmacists to have to make on any of the areas of the machine—EVER!!!! Jory insisted on this because many pharmacists like her were not mechanical. She often joked that all of her manuals said the same thing when she opened them up. The manuals instructions read, "Hey, Mason." Mason actually liked this joke. Although a joke, it was true. That was how Jory fixed everything by requesting Mason's talents. It worked every time. Mason was able to pull the "no adjustments" off, but it was a problem of great magnitude and extreme effort. If it could be done, Mason Gray could do it. The cell that would hold the medication was always the problem. The design was really hard to keep simple. Adjustments would have made it much, much easier. Previous companies had tried to automate to some degrees and had made the mistake of having adjustments. It was a major drawback.

CHICAGO

No matter how many miles they traveled their favorite trip was always to Graham Pharmaceutical in Chicago. Chicago became the "city of choice." They loved it. When it was just the two of them, they crammed in as much relaxing as possible when in the windy city. Long walks along Lake Shore drive with the Chicago wind blowing through their hair was a welcomed event. Michigan Avenue shopping, museums, The Aquarium, Navy Pier, trying to appear on the Oprah Winfrey show and all the Broadway plays were among the many attractions that lured them back to this beautiful city. Thanksgiving became a tradition for them to stay at the Stouffer Hotel on Wacker Drive. The hotel was beautiful and located where they could walk anywhere they wanted to go. This allowed them not to have to hassle with a car or taxi, which was a very attractive option. The ease of being close to everything made these trips what they were. It was a time to relax and get away from the constant hassles of owning their own fast paced, slow moving company. This time of year offered even more. The beautifully decorated city added to the spirit of the season. Marshall Field's decorated their windows with the animated

Christmas characters. Mickey Mouse, Dickens scenes, Pinocchio-all rented space in the large display windows that were housed in this seven story building for Christmas.

Movies were often being filmed in Chicago. One day in particular, Mason and Jory were walking along the cold, sunny Michigan Avenue approaching one of their favorite Star Bucks when the filming of a movie, starring Bruce Willis, halted them. Jory stopped cold in her tracks, dropping her jaw, as this was one of her favorite actors. She stood glued to her fraction of an inch space for hours to get a glimpse of Bruce. She actually did, and he ended up being only about ten feet from her. She would, from that point on, joke about how he came out of Star Bucks and waved at HER. When the movie was finally released, she told everyone SHE was in the movie and if one looked really hard through the windows of Star Bucks, she just might be seen. She absolutely loved this story and was thrilled to see her favorite movie star. Well, of course, turn about fair play. When Mason finally convinced Jory it was time to go and that was all there was to seeing Bruce, and "no," she couldn't touch, they walked away only to find another movie being filmed. Unfortunately for Jory this one was for Mason. Mason stopped cold in his tracks to watch a half-naked, big-boobed, blond dancing in the middle of Wacker Street. "Oh, brother Mason, some talent she is, **And, no**, those aren't real! Get a grip," she laughed.

With little interest in the woman, Jory watched the predominantly male crowd and giggled to herself at how they all were practically drooling watching this "actress." It reminded her of a joke Mason had told her about a web page that had described the difference between men and women. The man was illustrated as a "one switch" illustration while the woman was illustrated by having many switches and buttons. The complexity of the two boiled down to how many switches or buttons were involved. Obviously, this starlet had failed the "many switches" theory. The male crowd was proving the theory of the "one switch" to be correct. What kind of woman would go out half naked in the middle of Chicago and dance in the street? Obviously, one that was being paid very well. Mason and Jory spent about equal time between their movie stars and the day flew by. The days were always gone in a blink of an eye in beautiful Chicago. Walking back to the hotel the smell of caramel corn filled the entire seven hundred block of Michigan Avenue. Garrett's Popcorn was the culprit. This familiar smell routinely enticed Jory into buying the caramel corn. The smell was like a subliminal message. When the nose received the warm, buttery scent, one would drop anything to go straight to the counter and purchase the tasty, warm buttery corn. It didn't hurt that popcorn of any kind was one of Jory's favorite junk foods.

The day was evolving into evening when Mason and Jory returned to the hotel to get ready for an exhilarating evening out. The two went to a cozy restaurant they had heard a great deal about, Geja's Café. It was a romantic, dark, warm basement setting with soft Flamenco/Classical guitar music in the background. The fondue restaurant served six courses for the entire meal. The customers cooked all the courses themselves. It was luscious; Cheese fondues, vegetable fondue with beefy tan mushrooms, cherry red peppers, plump tomatoes, and subtle white onions. More food kept coming, constantly being served to each table. Shrimp fondue, chocolate fondue, everything fondue. What a fun dinner it was. The two were extremely and satisfyingly stuffed. They usually were only able to eat one meal a day because of how much each meal involved. Eating in Chicago was an event. They returned to the hotel fairly early and in Chicago, a stroll along Michigan Avenue into even the late hours was safe and was a worthy time. They strolled along the river, watching the tour boats float softly under the bridges, and chatted while the balmy air relaxed them. They went to the top floor of the Hancock building, which was home to a nightclub. They ordered drinks, visited with long conversations and mellowed out watching the city from the sky. Billowy clouds waved by the tops of the building as they were hundreds of feet up. They drank warm drinks and had warm conversation for about an hour before returning to the Stouffer. When they returned to the hotel in the evenings they would often go to the lobby where there was a pianist or a Jazz ensemble. One of Jory's favorite things in life was to sit and listen to piano music. The two sipped on their brandy and listened to the mellowing music until they both quieted and became sleepy. They left hand in hand, intertwined, relaxed and in love. These were much needed days splashed into their on going hectic lives. Chicago was an escape. It only added to the beauty of the city that it was easy to get to and a quick get away.

The meeting with Graham was encouraging. The people seemed genuine. It was an interesting place to visit. Graham and DII could not be any more different from one another, a new company and a conglomerate. Maybe it could work. After discussing options on how the two companies could work together it almost seemed doable. Mason was cautious but optimistic. Jory was elated to have the opportunity to be at Graham Pharmaceutical discussing their system.

They all left with good intentions and legal avenues were the next steps to explore. Time would tell with this adventure! Once all the legalities got underway, who knew what might surface? Until then, it was a viable option and an attractive one, at that.

DOTS

After a few days back into the rat race of the company, Mason needed some break time. It was very easy to get ran down on the schedule the Grays' were keeping. They lived their company. Every breath was now consumed by DII. DII had become their life. Now, what was needed were a few hours to regroup—just a few. That's all they could ask for or afford. A favorite past time was to watch movies. They didn't even have to be good movies just something to veg out with. Off Mason went to the nearest Blockbuster. As he was trying to decide between Matrix 2 and Red Planet, he was surprised to run into a former classmate, Dan Swythe. Dan was a stereotypical engineer, an academic type. He was a bearded, short, stocky, introverted man that lacked any social skills. Mason had classes with him, but the two were never friends, but rather academic acquaintances. The two had attended Kansas State University together when Mason was getting his Masters Degree in Mechanical Engineering. Dan had heard about Mason's invention and showed extreme enthusiasm. After an hour of reacquainting, Dan gave Mason a name of his brother-in-law, Derrik Peters. "Mason, I am serious, he is an accountant in Wichita and has many contacts that might be able to assist you in your endeavor," Dan explained with his subtle expression of excitement. Mason assumed it would probably be another dead end, but as he always did, he would check it out. He noticed the added exhaustion from all of the business chatter, and he ended up leaving Blockbuster without a movie. It was extremely difficult to get away from DII, both the location and the subject. As he was leaving he did manage to grab some "Dots" in the candy section. They were his favorite.

It was getting late and Mason felt the heaviness of the day taking over. As he got lost in his leather chair, bare feet up on his ottoman he pondered over the idea of actually making some kind of deal with someone he had somewhat of a connection to. This brought him some comfort, justified or not. There was, perhaps, a false sense of security adding on a partner locally verses the fear of a large corporation takeover. As he flipped the business card over and over between his fingers he kept seeing the name "Derrik Peters" appear and disappear. He had decided not to even mention this to Jory until he found out if it was real or not. He didn't like to get her hopes up to many times, for no reason, except to be disappointed. Tomorrow he would make the call. Maybe it would be the one. He wondered how many times he had this very same thought.

"Saturday would work fine, 9 o'clock," Mason reiterated. *Another viewing of the system to another potential interested party.* Derrik Peters would arrive in town on Saturday morning and come to DII to see Mason's creation. Mason always enjoyed showing off RxBot and knew if he did it often enough someone would be interested in investing and would actually show the money, rather than talk the money. Interest was never a problem, but actually seeing the bucks was another story. Mason was always up front about the company and the machine to potential investors. He knew the trouble it could bring if honesty wasn't totally revered even though most companies had lost that philosophy over the years. He informed Derrik of current problems and future plans for the system and made no excuses for the financial situation of the company. From the first day of incorporating, the Gray's had taken the advice of their attorneys and always followed the "full disclosure" rules. Obviously, this was attorney's advice and not the advice of businessmen. If investors had a true interest, there would be no questions as to a start up company having financial problems. To date, Mason knew of no companies that were rich from the very beginning. Not true, entrepreneurial, "start-up" companies.

After several hours of visiting and viewing RxBot and the technology, Derrik wanted to bring a friend and colleague back to see what he had seen and even visit the machine at John Crowe's pharmacy. Derrik had presented himself as a Certified Public Accountant and had many friends and investors he knew that liked to get involved in new companies such as DII. His friend, Matt Coggins was also a CPA and Matt new people that could bring in investment money. Derrik explained his involvement with Matt Coggins as being business partners from way back and currently had connections in all sorts of dealings together. Derrik presented an in depth resume which showed all of his current and past jobs as a CPA. It was impressive. Derrik had mentioned that if he could get things to work out he could see moving back to Manhattan since he was an avid "K-Stater" and had family in Manhattan. This was a pleasing thought to both of the Grays. The Grays had no desire to leave Manhattan. Derrik reassured Mason and Jory that he could get the money for DII to pay off their debt and to allow both Mason and Jory to be paid a reasonable salary. That thought alone, brought them both to a big subconscious sigh.

The next meeting involved Mason, Jory and Derrik to meet with Matt Coggins. Again, the meeting went better than expected. Mason explained the working RxBot system at John Crow's pharmacy. He told how accuracy was still a problem, but the new design of the cell that had taken an enormous amount of time was looking promising. Mason knew it was an overlooked statement by the non-engineering community, but he included how he intentionally made the design simple because if anyone understood the engineering behind this system they would appreciate the simplicity of the design. He explained how it was a major hurdle to keep it simple and that alone took tremendous time and effort. It frustrated Mason how people viewed that a simple design must not be as good as a complex design. If it's simple then it must be simple to design. The two, of course, are completely opposite. Mason had proven that the original design worked at the bench and at John Crowe's pharmacy. Improvements could always be made, but the core was good. Mason obviously demonstrated he was the technology of the system. He did, indeed, and now had behind him, the design and actual building of a new state of the art machine, the delivery, installation and service of a new machine and a new-patented product on the market. He had a great deal to offer. He truly was a brilliant engineer. Contracts were in hand to deliver five machines, but the company was out of money to go forward like it needed. It was fortunate that the Gray's had such a good relationship with all of their customers. The customers knew DII was a new company, but they would wait because they knew the system was something they really wanted. To this point, they too had an excitement to see this new product and company make it. So far, the customers indicated it would be worth the wait. All the legwork had been done and rapports established with the last five existing and the new five contracts. Mason, Matt and Derrik had all agreed that Matt and Derrik would talk to two of their wealthy friends about investing in DII, Jack Wilson III and Oscar Tyler. They both lived in Florida and were experienced investing buddies of Matts. Matt and Derrik often were Wilson and Tyler's spokespersons in most investment and business dealings. Mason had offered to call them himself or meet with them, but Matt and Derrik insisted that it would be best, at this point, if they did the leg work. If all went as planned, these new investors would pay off DII's debt, get money for salaries, move the company forward and Derrik Peters would move to Manhattan. Derrik and Matt didn't want payment for their services, but rather wanted interest in the company, as so many investors preferred. The meeting ended with everything happening very quickly. The only options DII had at this point was to do some sort of deal with Graham Pharmaceutical, with the fear of a takeover, or these new individuals, somewhat connected to Mason's past, although still strangers, but they had money and an interest to make this work. Mason and Jory were getting elated. Could it be *this* was it? This was actually going to happen. Both knew it probably wouldn't be as easy or go as smooth as it appeared, but it brought a welcomed optimism.

Mason and Jory were very optimistic, but still guarded with the meeting. Derrik and Matt appeared to be knowledgeable, connected individuals, but something about their demeanor made Jory uncomfortable. When she thought of Derrik's character she thought, *Squirrelly and a little shifty*, but she couldn't exactly put her finger on what bothered her. After all, one could be a keen business partner and still be "squirrelly" she supposed so she decided to blow off her instincts. When she thought of Matt's character, she felt confusion disconcerting, nothing she could put her finger on. It reminded her of some patients she had come in contact with at pharmacies. It was a red flag to her, but she could be very wrong. There was an extreme workload going on with forming this partnership and keeping DII on somewhat of a schedule. Prioritizing was the main priority. Deciding what was most important and what could be put to the side. Subconsciously, it slipped by and seemed unimportant to call any references on Derrik since he was, after all, a relative of a colleague. That fact had to count for something plus he had an overly impressive resume. At this point in the game, exhaustion many times interfered with judgment.

The next step was to take everyone to John Crowe's pharmacy in Salina, Kansas, and show them a working prototype. That is exactly what transpired. Everyone went except Oscar Tyler and Jack Wilson. Everything went well; the prototype hummed and showed its stuff. The proposed improvements to the next machine were pointed out on what was needed. Other than that, everyone seemed pleased and was ready to move on with getting this new partnership up and running.

Days were passing with constant communication between Mason, Jory, Derrik and Matt. DII needed a strong partner and details were being worked on to establish a working relationship between all of these individuals and DII investors. Could it be done? Mason and Jory were totally committed to their individual investors of DII. These were the people that took the greatest risk and believed in the two of them from the beginning. This was of utmost importance to remember. It wasn't a stumbling block, but it was a main issue to consider in forming a new alliance or partnership. Matt took it upon himself to inform Jack and Oscar of all the business dealings. Matt still felt it would be better for him to handle the details to his two close friends rather than Mason. This was a tad disconcerting, but at this point, somewhat reasonable. It appeared Matt and Derrik may have more financial savvy when dealing with investors, especially experienced investors. On the flip side, it became obvious, very quickly that their specialties were financial issues and not technical issues. Mason and Jory didn't need any more hats to wear. Their plate had been excessively full for the last four years. That's why this arrangement should be perfect. Now there would be specialists in different needed areas. Mason was uncomfortable with a partnership arrangement and preferred to have him and Jory act as consultants to eliminate the potential for a "conflict of interest" issue between DII and a new partnership. To form a new partnership and to maintain DII, would definitely be more difficult to manage. Mason and Jory would have to be involved in both companies if that were the path to follow. Matt felt that there was no "conflict of interest" issue and felt the partnership was a better business decision. DII board of directors met constantly with attorneys and among themselves to insure the safest and most profitable way to pursue. Derrik felt the Grays could indeed act as consultants and he still would prefer to move to Manhattan. How was all of this going to be decided? Money certainly would have the final say, no doubt, since that is how it worked. Mason and Jory alone, with their blood sweat and tears, had put in about seventy thousand dollars into DII before meeting up with Matt and Derrik. This was a huge amount of money for a couple that started with one little idea and limited funds, both personally and professionally. Neither Grays, nor DII had any more money to put into a partnership or even the legalities of it. Coggins and Peters were very aware of this fact and assured everyone involved that it wouldn't be a problem once they recruited Wilson and Tyler to join this new venture. Matt and Derrik would not be putting any money in either.

Only a few quick weeks passed working on all sorts of details. Between meetings, excitement was at an all time high. The Grays couldn't expend energy at a faster rate. It was truly incredible to realize one could find this much energy when pursuing a dream. Finally, the meeting to put it all together was scheduled. Matt Coggins had his own legal arrangements for what looked like a new partnership. Matt despised lawyers and felt he was knowledgeable enough to write most of the contract without legal advice. It was such a welcomed arrangement because legal fees could eat the company's lunch, in an afternoon. Trust was growing, between the four at a rapid rate due to the amount that needed to be done to form some kind of working relationship. DII attorneys were involved, but in a decreasing rate due to the financial status of DII, but still encouraged the company to go forward with a partnership as a Limited Liability Corporation, the "LLC" with these four new individuals. It did however, still cost a fortune for DII, but just not as big of a fortune with Matt doing most of the legal footwork. There was such an incredible amount of work to be done with forming this alliance and keeping DII moving on a day to day basis that delegation continued at an all time high. Let each person take care of his or her own specialty. It was the only way to get it even close to all done. The concerns Mason and Jory had about Matt and Derrik were buried in their subconscious due to the work loads and deadlines to be met. Trust was all there was time for. What other attractive offers, actual offers, did they have at that moment? To be able to fulfill their contractual obligations with the next five machines was their number one goal and the option to form the LLC was pushing them in that direction.

HIDDEN WOLF

Saturday morning, the air was frigid, but the sun was bright. The day had promise. Mason and Jory traveled to Matt Coggins office in Wichita, Kansas. Mason, Jory, Derrik, and Matt were all going to meet with Wilson and Tyler on a conference call to set up all the remaining details of forming the LLC. Mason and Jory arrived and got an uneasy feeling as they walked up to Coggin's CPA office that looked like a gingerbread house. Mason and Jory had every emotion brewing that could be possible at any one time. Excitement of course, apprehension and nervousness were swimming inside both of them. Before leaving their truck Mason turned to Jory and requested, "A kiss for luck?"

Jory abided by the offer and responded, "Our roller coaster looks like we are leveling out for once!"

They both jumped out of the truck and went into the building. As they entered, both noticed a mismatched, uncomfortable look, but it was obviously done with effort. One could tell there was an amount of money put into the decor that would compare to a political campaign. An inadequate design though, with a decor that belonged to a cutesy kitchen, but then would abruptly change into a room filled with solid mahogany conference tables. Marble accents splashed throughout the room to complete the corporate aura. The lighting was dim, and the dark rooms somewhat hazy from cigarette smoke. One felt confused from the presentation of the place, but maybe it was because it was so obvious a ton of money had to be spent on this place that it made it seem successful somehow. It was an out of place adornment—a weird twist. Jory thought to herself, *Can a place be ominous and successful?* When Mason and Jory entered, the first office belonged to Susan Coggins, CPA, Matt's, wife. A nice enough woman, but she had a weird demeanor. She was bold, and had an immediate appearance of being bossy. However, putting all personalities aside, everything could still work. These people after all didn't have to be friends just business partners.

Small chatter took about fifteen minutes and Matt, Derrik, Mason and Jory finally met in Matt's comfortable office, which was actually right off of the real "cutesy" kitchen. The walls of this fifty two year olds office were covered with prizes, trophies and pictures of prized winning horses. This office made a statement—comprised of mahogany woods, marble floors, expensive fixtures and paintings. One could tell that only the best and most expensive was what made up this "accounting firm." Subconsciously, Jory noticed the "Bev Doolittle" prints being the main decor of Coggins' office. One in particular the "Hidden Wolf" haunted her as she faced the dark wall. Unknown to her, these prints would be one of Matt's prized possessions and be referred to numerous times for the hidden pictures. Jory couldn't put her finger on it, but the pictures described how she was feeling abut her new business partners. Maybe she wasn't seeing the real picture. Something seemed hidden, but she again attributed it to being cautious of the cardinal rule, "Trust no one and remain majority stock holders." The hours were passing and ideas were being written down by all on how to proceed. Oscar and Jack ended up not being available for the planned conference call after all. It was explained that after talking to Matt they didn't feel a need for much due diligence and would agree to whatever Matt decided. This made Mason and Jory a bit uncomfortable, but eventually bought into the trust. A rough draft from the notes would be presented to the attorneys to see if the partnership could work. Both sides had done their homework on how it could be done. At the end of the day, it was decided the paperwork would be presented to Matt Coggins' attorneys. They would write it up and then DII attorneys, to shorten the amount of time DII attorneys would have to charge, would review it. An arrangement of a Limited Liability Corporation was the final plan. DII attorney involvement reassured Mason and Jory on trusting the LLC option. Matt Coggins proposed for himself, and on behalf of Jack Wilson and Oscar Tyler, that he would be Secretary/Treasurer, and manager for the LLC. Matt indicated again he didn't want involved in the day-to-day activities, and that he didn't want compensation other than part ownership in the LLC. The LLC would pick up associated costs with all the money that would be invested by Wilson and Tyler. The only money put into the LLC would be by Wilson and Tyler and this was agreed upon by all. What a deal. It was next to being too good to be true. Matt Coggins said numerous times, he always wanted a company "like this" and what a deal since he wasn't putting any investment money into the LLC. Once the LLC was formed, the arrangement involved Mason as President of the LLC; Jory would be a consultant since she was working at the pharmacy and at DII. Matt and Derrik would be managers and provide financial expertise, but not on a day-to-day basis. The equity structure would provide a balance of power, with no single individual having absolute control. Wilson and Tyler would be voting as independents. Originally it was proposed that the LLC would consist of Mason owning forty percent, Derrik twelve percent and Matt eight percent with forty percent set aside for additional investors. If this would not have been the case then the new partners would have sixty percent to control the partnership and Mason was not eager to relinquish control. On top of all this good news, it was decided that once a new machine was built the first one would go to John Crowe to replace his prototype, which had already gone above and beyond its limits. This was a huge relief since John had devoted himself and invested a great deal into DII. It was also decided that John Crowe should serve as a major player in the newly formed LLC. Aside from the original discussion on the structure it was decided that Wilson and Tyler, John Crowe and Jory would all be part of the LLC. Mason would split his equity to provide ownership to John and Jory.

It only took a couple of days before the legalities were finished and there was a newly formed Limited Liability Corporation. Mason, President and Manager, Derrik, Chief Operating Officer (which was slightly puzzling since he wasn't going to be involved on a day to day basis) and Manager, Matt, Secretary/Treasurer, Manager and advisor without compensation and daily involvement. Matt was excited to finally be involved in the company of his dreams so no one objected to the added advisor title. Mason and Derrik would be salaried. Jory would still act as a consultant since she would continue to be Vice President of DII and continued to work at the pharmacy. She would remain the sales and marketing contact for both companies and she would be paid a set amount for consulting on a part-time basis. The new LLC did in fact pay some of DII's existing debt and made it workable by calling it Advanced Royalties. It was going to be nice having a CPA that knew how to do all the financial details. Initially, it was decided that DII would have a fifty thousand dollar line of credit, secured by the patent awarded on the system and the note being a three-year note. This all sounded fair and doable. Attorneys on both sides worked out the details with a workable legal agreement for all parties involved and for both the LLC and DII. When it was time to sign all the documents, all were signed with the exception of a typographical error on the "line of credit" document, reading fifteen thousand instead of fifty thousand. This too, had been discussed and in time would be corrected and signed by all.

There were some details that needed worked out and a few did create some difficulties. Matt insisted that most of the work be done out of his office in Wichita. He felt for financial reasons the LLC should run out of his accounting firm. It was still an acceptable option for Mason to continue to live in Manhattan and run both DII and the LLC. He would commute to Wichita for a couple of years. It was "only" a two-hour commute. Matt told Mason he would get him an apartment so he could work out of it, if and when Mason needed it. Derrik decided to stay in Wichita at this point. DII already had a customer base and a toll free telephone number in Manhattan that was printed on all the marketing materials. The phone could ring either in Wichita or Manhattan even if it was a Manhattan number due to the call forwarding option. The bills were established in DII's name and it was decided by all involved parties that it would remain that way. The LLC would provide money to pay all bills, the LLC's and DII's.

The next meeting was to determine a name for the newly formed LLC. Matt was determined to make the name of the company the same as the product. There was some hesitation among the others, but Matt seemed to be the one that had an agenda for how the LLC should go and to this point there seemed no harm in naming the LLC, RxBot, LLC. DII already had a licensed trademark name RxBot for the machine. Susan joined in with her opinions, which was turning into a daily event. Susan was the stereotypical, fifty-year-old, menopausal, pushy woman. She bluntly agreed that the name should be what Matt thought it should be. It became obvious very quickly that Matt liked to think ideas were his. This too, still seemed harmless enough. It was a known fact that many keen business managers had huge egos to go along with their positions. A lot of work had been accomplished and everyone definitely needed a break by this time. The whole group followed Matt's direction in suggesting a favorite deli down the street for a late lunch. This place had been an old time favorite sandwich shop of the Coggins'. Everyone ordered and Matt subtly asked Mason if he would pay for it on the DII American Express card until a new line of credit could be established for the newly formed LLC.

"Not a problem," Mason agreed.

While waiting for their sandwich orders, personal conversations took place to loosen up everyone and to try to get to know each other on a different level. Mason and Jory told of how they got together and how they got to this point of starting their own company along with some outside interests interjected in. Susan complained that Matt didn't need more to do, but again mentioned how he always wanted a company like RxBot, LLC. She explained how he already had sleep disorders and had to sleep with tennis balls in his shirt so he could breathe. The tennis balls would make him sleep in the right position or so the theory was explained. Matt said his anxiety sometimes got the best of him. Derrik joked and said, "Or his paranoia." This new group tended to lean towards "odd", but so far nothing insurmountable; in fact it just added to the interest. Up to this point, Mason and Jory had already felt they had seen it all. Mason and Jory would throw each other understood glances of humor and inquisitive expressions.

After another long day, Mason and Jory returned to Manhattan only to be greeted by their good and loyal friend, Hobbes. Mason decided to call his life long and best friend, Seth Seagal, while Jory took Hobbes for their evening walk. Seth was a brilliant man that remained a faithful and dedicated friend to Mason throughout the years. Seth was an aeronautical engineering graduate of Massachusetts Institute of Technology and received a Masters in Business Administration from the University of Chicago and had many keen ideas on how a business should be run. He was an extremely interesting individual that always came through with good advice to Mason. After an hour of catching up, Seth had many good ideas for Mason, one of which to remain cautious, but overall it could be an arrangement that could work. Mason certainly had a mind of his own, but took Seth's advice very seriously. Together they were quite a team. Seth wanted to know what Jory's opinion was as he was always interested in what she thought. Seth and Jory were very different individuals, but there was a mutual interest and respect in what each other thought over the years. Mason explained that Jory was extremely excited about having some options, but remained very guarded, at this point. Overtime, they continuously bounced ideas off one another about various subjects. Seth and Mason talked for about an hour before agreeing to visit at a later date. There was never enough time for their visits. Everything was happening at such a rapid rate that Mason didn't want to overlook anything. It was impossible to know what every move should be, but if enough brilliant people got together then chances were far greater for success. Mason was so hoping that all the people on board were trustworthy and as competent as they appeared. He was convinced he only had one choice and that was to keep on moving. He had become extremely excited that everything was falling into place. His judgment, possibly was impaired or perhaps even improved, with all of the excitement. With all the activities it would be hard to tell, either way.

Jory returned with Hobbes from their comfortable, calming walk. She and Mason were visiting when they heard a ruckus outside. Four small boys were playing hide and seek out in the front neighbor's yard. The rules of the game required some footing on the Gray's yard. When Mason went outside, after hearing the ruckus, Hobbes barked, jumped and darted out the front door. He used his mean sounding bark only to find four little boys suspended in air from fright of the "ferocious" dog. The small playful boys had chosen one of the Gray's vehicles to hide behind and when Hobbes figured this out he literally scared the pee out of them. The kids screamed at the top of their lungs and all legs and hands were suspended in the air and there couldn't have been a dry pair of pants on any one of them when they scampered off to safety. Mason and Jory were laughing so hard from the display of these children, that they too about wet their pants. Unknown to the little boys, Hobbes barked because he knew something out of the ordinary was going on, but when he saw the kids he just wanted to play. The jumping and screaming only added to Hobbes' assurance that it was playtime. After all, could anyone really be afraid of Mr. Hobbes. Needless to say, Hobbes strutted back to the house with a smile a mile wide and "tail a wagging." His job was done for the night—perimeter secured!

The next few weeks involved transferring all information from DII to RxBot, LLC. Everything was transferred. Everything. Matt continued to insist that everything be done in his office since he had the personnel for it. All of the files on DII customers were taken over to Matts and copied. Mason constantly worked on the manufacturing details of the machine. He was extremely busy with his areas and relieved to have new people for all the different areas. Being so tied up with manufacturing he didn't have a minute to spare to oversee any of the other areas. Contracts still had to be honored and in the time frame DII had originally given to their customers. Meetings with potential employees also took much of the time. Matt and Derrik, being located in Wichita, knew of many professional people that may be interested in joining the RxBot team. A meeting with Scott Thomas was in the works to bring on an additional marketing professional. Why the need for more marketing people, at this point was somewhat questionable, even though customer interest or especially because customer interest was at an all time high. Assuming the LLC had to start somewhere perhaps marketing personnel was as good as any place to start. Matt didn't seem concerned about finances so everyone agreed it would be all right to look at hiring additional marketing personnel. Everyone could use extra help in all areas due to the workload ahead of the whole company. DII and its counterpart, RxBot, LLC, were up and going and there was a future for both in progress.

There was a continued push to meet the deadlines for one of the next five machines, an HMO contract. A meeting to see their purchased machine was sat up for May and Matt and Derrik were never happy with the contract DII had made with them. They did however, agree to honor the contract. They felt the price was to low. Numerous times they mentioned finding a way to raise it. The HMO originally received a "good deal" because they were one of the first customers for a "real" machine and not a prototype. They were willing to wait and deal with the imperfections of a newly formed company and product. Mason stood on firm ground and would not let any of the contract be changed due to this fact and his loyalty to them. If the HMO was willing to believe in them at this point, then they should receive something for their patience and loyalty. It seemed the first few customers were as excited about this new company and its history and product as the people that were actually involved in the development of all it.

INTERFERENCE

A couple of months passed and there was tremendous effort to get designs to subcontractors that Matt knew. Matt would only use subcontractors that he had connections with. There just wasn't time to bicker about Matt's ego and what the intent was to use only his people. He appeared to know what he was doing at this point, in the financial end of the business and the delegation helped get things accomplished. As far as his non-involvement in day-to-day activities, it just wasn't happening. As he became more involved he became more of a nuisance. And was he ever involved. His lack of knowledge in anything technical was a big problem and a huge obstacle. Mason was spending more and more time trying to explain to Matt why the cell did NOT need to be redesigned, why the software did NOT completely need reworked and the vial handlers did NOT need to be redesigned. What it basically boiled down to was that if Matt didn't have a person of his own on the project then it needed reworked. Matt, had a brother-in-law, Sam Stevens, that he insisted using and it was killing him to not have him doing the software. DII had hired one of the best software guru's, Tim Larue, in the country and was a friend to Mason. He had worked on the RxBot machine software for years. He could fix and create anything. The software was dynamic and did constantly need additions and deletions, but between Tim and Mason the machine could do just about everything, but sing. It was entertaining to watch. This was starting to become a point of contention with Matt because he really wanted his brother-in-law Sam involved. Many times, Matt was so fixated on this point. Days were spent trying to convince him not to change what wasn't broken or what didn't need to be fixed. There were tremendous deadlines approaching that had to be met and with using everything that worked already it would still be hard to meet them all. Mason was getting very frustrated trying to pacify Matt. Of course, whatever Matt wanted, his shadow, Derrik was right there grinning and agreeing. It was obvious that high tech was not the specialty of either of these accountants. They were becoming like two bulls in a china cabinet.

    Matt deviated a tad, from trying to redesign what worked. He wanted RxBot to use his new software that his accounting firm had purchased and to get DII to download their Parts List to his location. This too, took a tremendous amount of Mason's time. He did just enough every day on these issues to pacify Matt because it was obvious he wouldn't let the subjects rest. It was as if he was obsessive compulsive on his ideas. Mason knew it was important to try to keep harmony between all of them because with as much work as there was to get done there just wasn't time for unrest between any of them.

    Baby-sitting however, couldn't take up the whole day, every day.

    Nathan Roule had been hired by DII and had become Mason's right hand engineer for about two years before the LLC was formed. He helped with all the designs and had learned the machine inside and out. Mason relied on him. Matt was unsettled with the relationship between Mason and Nathan. Matt wanted control. Derrik wanted control. He would make comments to Nathan that it was hard to "control" Mason. He said it reminded him of his son because he had trouble controlling him too. Mason never understood what that was supposed to mean or how it entered into any of the working equations. This was somewhat unnerving to Mason, but again there just wasn't time to worry about this sort of thing. Whenever Nathan was in Wichita and not around Mason, Matt would insist Nathan give Matt anything he had, manuals, download software, everything. He wanted all DII information in any way, shape or form.

A COLD DAY IN MARCH

There were months of non-stop work and tension mounting. It was an extremely cold day in March when it was obvious everyone needed a break. Matt came into Derrik's office where Mason and Jory were meeting with Derrik. Matt suggested everyone take a break and go to his horse farm for the rest of the afternoon. As strange as this seemed, it didn't sound half bad. Derrik didn't go, but Susan, Mason, Jory and Matt all went. Matt and Susan took Mason and Jory to their home and let them borrow a few clothes so they could go to the horse farm. The afternoon was eliminating time, but by late afternoon they all arrived at Coggins horse farm. It was amazing. The horses were beautiful and the farm was humongous with an equally large staff. Feeling extremely troubled by the tour they took and how much of DII'S things were in Matt's sheds; they followed his lead and took it all in, not knowing what it all meant. They both felt a sense of confusion. The horse staff knew how to do cabling with the machines and how to do some assembling. Mason didn't understand exactly what the horse farm or Matt's staff exactly had to do with either company, but Matt explained since he had the resources he just used them and the space to cut costs. Matt interrupted Mason from his building anxiety, suggesting he climb up on the horse and go for a ride. It was so unbelievably cold Mason and Jory would do anything to try to stay warm. The extreme cold was unusual for March, but old man winter wasn't going out without a fight this year. They were using borrowed clothing and had limited warm articles. Mason and Jory rode for a short time and then the rest of the day watched Matt and Susan ride. It was so cold that both Mason and Jory had lost all feeling in their hands and feet. It was uncomfortable enough that the thought of frostbite had actually become a reality. Matt and Susan were in no hurry to end the riding sessions since they were dressed appropriately. Finally, the sun was setting to a most spectacular sunset. Another, spilled paint can full of oranges, pinks and blues thrown randomly in the sky—absolutely gorgeous. The extreme cold clear days of Kansas usually ended in a sunset that was memorable. By this time, Matt and Susan were acting really strange, even more than usual. They were distant, but finally returned Mason and Jory to their hotel after several miserable cold hours. Mason and Jory were starting to ignore these moods of Matt and Susan and resigning to the fact they were just two strange ducks. After Mason and Jory were dropped off at their hotel they were frozen near death, so they felt. Exhaustion came over them from the bitter cold that they both fell asleep without dinner and without removing a stitch of clothing, coats and all. They snuggled like never before to keep warm. This was a huge statement since they were very good at snuggling under even normal circumstances. It was the coldest day either of them could remember. Matt and Susan didn't consider helping them obtain anything to keep them warm or at least shorten the horse riding. Subconsciously, it seemed to be some sort of message in showing Mason and Jory just who exactly was in charge. Both, Mason and Jory became increasingly unsettled, but there was nothing they could do but keep moving forward.

DOUBLETREE HOTEL

It was a Tuesday evening and Mason and Jory wanted to call it quits so they could get back to Manhattan at a decent time. The coming weekend was the national pharmacy meeting in Orlando, Florida that they both would be attending. Jory attended these meetings every year, but this year would be a work meeting to try to get new customers and to spread the word around about RxBot. Besides the trip including work, Mason and Jory were looking forward to the escape and the reacquainting with their friend Seth. Actual, "in-person" visits were few and far between with Seth, but that didn't seem to matter because they often picked up where they had left off. Seth lived in Miami and would travel to Orlando to spend some time with Mason and Jory. It had been a long time since they had a chance to get together. Jory was anxious to talk to Seth as she was feeling uncomfortable about many of the work issues that were falling in front of her these days. She figured most of her uneasiness must be from exhaustion, but nevertheless a good long conversation with Seth would be helpful, she hoped. It had only been a few months since the forming of the LLC, but she felt very uncomfortable about many issues and was really starting to regret not paying more attention to those red flags she felt in the beginning of the relationship. She still was optimistic it was just personality differences, but her gut was telling her something different.

As Mason was packing up tools and such to return to Manhattan, Matt called and was in a panic. For some reason he wanted to call an emergency meeting at the Doubletree Hotel with Derrik, Mason, Jory and himself. Mason was actually quite disgusted, but agreed and would try to cut it short. He knew of no emergencies and couldn't get much out of Matt to explain the urgency, but nonetheless they would all meet.

There were only about thirty minutes before Matt wanted them to meet and most of that time would be used in traveling to the restaurant. Mason and Jory were unsettled about the meeting, but tried to comply with whatever they could, and in fact, they went out of their way, most of the time. Once they got to the restaurant both wondered subconsciously how come Matt always picked the most expensive places to eat. After all it was a business meeting and we were still a new company on a limited budget Matt probably knew how to use his accounting expertise to get every dime back anyway so no one ever said much about that issue. Matt was determined to discuss business the whole time and he wanted everyone, excluding himself to give up some portion of their ownership to bring his brother-in law on board to redo the software. Matt insisted that since Mason and Jory owned the largest amount of equity that they should give up eight percent to bring on his brother in law, Sam Stevens to redo the software. Here he was back to bringing his brother-in-law into the company. This man was not going to let this subject drop until he got what he wanted. "After all, Mason you know the core of the software is bad," Matt said nonchalantly like Mason would understand what he was talking about.

Mason, confused, asked Matt, "What the hell are you talking about the core is bad? I totally disagree and, Matt, how many times are we going to have to go over this?"

Matt's face was turning red as he hated when anyone doubted his limited knowledge. And was it ever limited. Matt convincingly added, "John Crowe also stated the software was bad."

Mason knew that this wasn't a true statement and gave a puzzling look. "Matt, I think you misunderstood John on that matter."

"Oh, no there was no misunderstanding he wants us to redo the software and he wants my brother-in-law to do it," Matt reiterated.

Mason and Jory were not interested in this whole conversation and as politely as possible let it known. That didn't matter because Matt and Derrik were not going to lighten up on the matter.

Mason went back to the equity issue to try to divert a tad, "Ya know if there is more equity needed then everyone should put some in since everyone would supposedly benefit."

Matt, increasingly getting more nervous, stated, "No, that won't work!" Mason also threw in that it was time he visited with Tyler and Wilson.

Matt jumped on that issue so fast that if he would have fallen off his chair it wouldn't have been a surprise. "Mason, if you contact them, then I will apologize on your behalf!"

"Apologize on my behalf? God, Matt, what are you talking about?" Mason asked inquisitively. It was as if someone waved a gigantic red flag on the table in front of Mason and Jory. This comment could not mean anything good. Mason moved on as he didn't want to give this the time it needed right at that moment.

"Matt, there has got to be more structure to the decision making in this organization. One person needs to orchestrate engineering." Mason thought this was a reasonable way to go since he was President and the one engineer that did truly know the machine inside and out. It just seemed obvious. Mason talked until he was blue in the face how it would be a huge mistake to scrap all of the software at this point and start over. He again, never felt that the software couldn't be improved, but to scrap it completely was ridiculous.

Mason asked, "And what about Tim?" He had always done a great job with the software and had been with Mason for years. Was Mason supposed to just get rid of him because Matt wanted his brother-in-law to start over?

The pressure from Matt mounted all through dinner. His demeanor was condescending and insinuating that Mason had no right to disagree with him especially after what all Matt felt he had done for RxBot. The conversation went on for what seemed like an eternity and absolutely nothing was decided. The dinner sucked right along with the company and the conversation. At this point, it was hard to say what Matt had done except get in the way of progress. The meeting was very uncomfortable and accomplished nothing but ill will. This could only mean there would be another emergency meeting in the near future. Matt obsessed over everything until he finally felt he was getting his way. It was becoming clearer there was something wrong with Matt. Jory was convincing herself it was possibly a medical condition and even if it wasn't, it was certainly abnormal behavior. Jory was looking so forward to that trip to Orlando and visiting with Seth. It couldn't happen fast enough. She kept finding herself drifting to this thought to help her maintain her self-control through this idiotic conversation. It took incredible effort to pacify huge egos. The night ended with DII picking up the tab as Matt didn't have any of RxBot, LLC credit cards with him, again. This was becoming a real pet peeve of Jorys. So far it hadn't really created too much of a problem, but somehow it still bothered her. RxBot, LLC paid the bills at the end of the month, only after Jory was scrutinized over every item and with everything explained by her until she couldn't explain anymore. Even this was all right with her since it made her feel like Matt was watching the finances in everyone's best interest. Matt wanted to know where and why money was being spent. In all fairness, a company needed that. It was agreed Matt would generate monthly financial reports and each partner would receive them. At least she could keep tabs, too.

FRIENDSHIPS

It was a pretty, sunny morning in Orlando as they must all be. Seth would be arriving around noon and then all three of them would go out for lunch. Mason and Jory were glad to get away from RxBot, LLC for a little while. It was time to regroup. Jory got up at six o'clock to hit some of the first continuing education lectures so she could make her stay worthwhile. After all, in the afternoon and evening she would want to play so she was paying the price early for that playtime later. A continuing education would start her day with breakfast and a slide tour through the Amazon rain forest at seven. Although early, it was a topic Jory extremely enjoyed and wished she could visit the laboratory of the rainforests herself someday. She figured there must be an unlimited amount of medications contained in those places. It was a horticulturist's, pharmacist's playground.

It was awesome to see Seth again. Time passed between the three of them chatting and discussing as if they had truly picked up where they had left off from the previous time. The evening had a promise of fun, excitement and good ole friendship lined up. The three went out to dinner at The Crabhouse Seafood Restaurant to eat their favorite seafood. The conversation was more serious than any of them had hoped for. True feelings were put on the table about RxBot, LLC. Mason, as always, was optimistic and trusting, but something happened to Jory in this conversation. It was as if she hadn't had anyone to talk to for a very long time outside of RxBot, LLC. For the first time, it became obvious that she and Mason's roads were not parallel. They were dividing on ideas. Mason was always the trusting soul and Jory the skeptic. Most of the time it worked to their advantage to have each one on the opposite side. She explained to Seth that she had inklings of bad feelings about the partnership and where it was headed. Seth being his level headed self, wanted to know details. After a couple of hours of chatting, Jory could see the concern in Seth's eyes and the trustingness in Mason's. Somehow none of this made Jory feel any better maybe, in fact, worse to see a possible division between Mason and her on the opinions of the new partners. It could only mean trouble.

Jory hurriedly changed the subject, "Well, enough of this seriousness, let's go to Universal Studios." And that's what they did.

It was raining, but none of them cared. The first thing the three of them did was ride "Back to the Future." Now, if that wasn't worth the whole trip, nothing was. Riding in a Dilorian could make any troubles go away. It was hysterical and all three laughed harder than any of them could remember for quite some time. Seth, too, needed a break as he was always working on some new ideas and consulting. He was trying to start his own business and his life wasn't any less stressful than the Grays'. The night offered long conversations and reacquainting that was well needed.

After Universal Studios, the three were totally soaked from the drenching rain and Seth already was coming down with a serious cold. All three went back to the hotel bar had some drinks and listened to music. They visited with constant input from each friend. Seth quietly in a middle of other conversations mentioned his girlfriend, Pam had died. He just threw in this incredible information like it was just normal conversation. Pam had touched Seth's heart, which so few women could do. This was startling to Mason and Jory, too, as they had met her and felt she was a good match for him as well as a great person. Apparently, she died in her home somehow, suddenly and unexpectedly. It was obviously on Seth's mind, but not enough to elaborate. Mason and Jory were caught off guard and didn't know how to respond. The evening got late and all relaxed to the music and the influence of alcohol, into wee hours of the morning. The conversations got slower and softer until the evening had dawned a new day.

The trip was over and so quickly. It was time to return to the RxBot rat race. Seth, Mason and Jory visited every minute they could and explored Orlando on limited time. It was sad to say goodbye. Goodbyes usually meant years would go by before all would get together again. Mason and Jory got on the plane and were both really tired from the schedule they had kept in Orlando. Jory was drifting off as the plane was taking off and about fifteen minutes into the flight, she thought she saw a bright light as the plane began to fall and took a really sharp turn. She knew what turbulence felt like and it didn't feel like this. She woke up abruptly and grabbed Mason's hand. She and Mason's knuckles were white and she heard other people screaming including the baby behind her.

Once the plane regained its composure the pilot came on over the intercom and said, "I apologize for that maneuver, but I chose to miss the other plane!"

Jory couldn't believe it. Up to this point, she had loved to fly. She was one who had loved the thunderstorms and wanted planes to fly as close as possible—not anymore. This changed everything. She began to cry from the fear. She realized that when airplanes crashed, the frightened passengers probably know what is going on for most of the fall. The fall of this plane couldn't have been more than mere seconds, but it seemed like a lifetime and it almost was. She wanted off the plane, but of course they still had two long hours to go. After several stiff drinks, Kansas City International finally came into sight. Everyone on the plane was tense from the flight and relieved to see the final destination. Mason stayed calm and cool about the incident, but Jory didn't. As the pilot approached Kansas City, a storm had begun and rain was hitting the plane. Jory didn't want close to this thunderstorm. The plane was just about to land when it sped up, climbing, when it should be touching down.

"That's it!" Jory exclaimed. "We're close enough, I'll just jump out. Let me out of this plane!"

The storm had caused the pilot to circle and re-approach the landing for some reason. Probably a reason Jory didn't want to know. The plane did finally arrive safely and none too soon. Everyone looked relieved to be on the ground and to be safe. This flight changed Jory's whole perspective on flying. She would avoid it if she could.

Not only did it seem their roller coaster was in a descent, but the life around them was taking on that same appearance. It felt like there was a storm brewing and not just the one outside of the plane. It felt bad, wrong, and threatening.

DETERIORATION

Once they returned, April arrived trying to be as fresh as spring. Deadlines were approaching rapidly and interference from Derrik and Matt was beginning to seem intentional and malicious. Mason started delaying his calls back to them since they had become such a nuisance and hindering any progress. What exactly was going on? Did they want the deadlines to be met or not? It was hard to say. It seemed like for some unknown reason, they wanted to halt progress. Something was definitely wrong.

Jory continued her morning walks with Hobbes, every morning, rain, snow, sleet or hail, but this morning was fog. The fog was intensely thick. She was aware of how symbolic the fog was to her life lately. Nothing was clear anymore. She could only see maybe ten feet in front of her. Somehow it was comforting as she felt surrounded by a peacefulness, which allowed her to contemplate many details for the entire walk. She had successfully made it up and over "dead dog hill"! The hill was named by Mason and Jory because it was such an intense hill to walk and they always felt like "dead dogs" after completing it. Involved in her own thoughts and Hobbes off enjoying his adventure, she looked up and right in front of her, within reach, was a fawn. It was only because visibility was next to nothing that the fawn allowed Jory to get this close. It was an awesome experience. It brought a much needed calmness and smile. For a brief second, both caught each other's eyes, then off went the fawn, feeling safe enough, but nonetheless left.

As Jory predicted, Matt called another emergency meeting on the software issue. Before the meeting Mason, Jory, and Derrik had all decided that everyone would put up some equity equally, to bring on Sam, to "help" with software improvements. The equity split would include Matt this time, and then the issue could be dealt with. Mason agreed to this so he could get Derrik and Matt off his back. This would allow him to proceed with the manufacturing of the "state of the art machine" that so badly demanded his time and attention. That's all Mason wanted, to work on his invention and to bring it to fruition. Matt's brother-in-law, Sam, would perhaps have a place for upgrades when bells and whistles were needed. For now the software was "user-friendly," simple and it worked. This is what was needed to get the next five machines on the market. The three decided this would work and Derrik would get Matt to also agree. The meeting time actually ended up getting delayed due to everyone's demanding schedule. Derrik sent a memo to Mason and Jory to indicate what had been discussed by him, Mason and Jory, about everyone putting in some equity.

Jory heard the fax machine crackling its normal routine. After she retrieved the fax, she felt her face heating up and yelled for Mason. "Mason come quick, you have to see this!" The memo stated nothing of the actual conversation and asked for signatures to the release equity of Mason, Jory and John Crowe, to be given to Matt Coggins' brother-in-law so the software could be *started*. Mason was livid. This would be the memo that changed the trust level between all parties from here on out. Mason tried to get some kind of understanding from Derrik, but failed miserably.

Derrik told Mason, "Just sign it. You can get out of anything!"

Mason had gotten used to never knowing what Derrik was up to other than following Matt's direction. What was actually going on was unclear, but it was clear something was. Mason immediately wrote back a memo and called a meeting with all parties. The meeting actually happened and Derrik and Matt gave face-to-face apologies. Peculiar as it was, it did give some sense of relief, but still the trust level had decreased.

Jory also asked Matt if it was just a misunderstanding about the whole software issue. Did he really not understand the technology well enough to understand that the existing software did work and that it worked well?

He admitted, "I just don't understand the software."

Jory thought that was the first logical statement he had made in a long time and she felt some relief. Just maybe all the talking and discussing had paid off. Maybe they were getting through to Matt. This could draw an end to the software issue and then everyone could finally move on. It should have anyway.

TORNADIC

A blast from a sauna couldn't have been more stifling than the blast of humid air that hit Jory's face when she opened the door to the new morning. It was the kind of day that had ominous written all over it. It was hot, humid and not an extra molecule of air to spare. The weather was brewing in its own turmoil. The day had a full schedule with no extra minutes to spare as every day had become. Today was going to prove to be another long drawn out day. The day would start with another meeting with Derrik and some of the existing investors of DII in Topeka then traveling again to Wichita to work with Scott on marketing issues. The day would confirm, as they all did, to be long, hard and tense. After spending the afternoon in Topeka discussing the horrifying topic "again" that the company was "out of money" *again*, according to Derrik and Matt, it was decided to approach DII's investors for additional moneys. Matt and Derrik consistently convinced Mason, Jory and investors that they themselves didn't need to invest actual money because they were not getting compensation in the capacity needed for their expertise, which had some logic to it. Apparently forgotten was the fact they weren't going to be compensated because they weren't supposed to be involved in the day to day operations. After the meeting in Topeka, they all returned to the Wichita office.

Jory went by the office to pick up the monthly financial report as she did every month. She approached Derrik's office and heard Derrik and Scott discussing something in somewhat quiet voices, anyway, not in their normal tone. She poked her head into the office, energetic as usual, saying, "Hi guys!" startling the two hushed men. Odd as this seemed, she reassured herself to keep calm and to wait patiently. She felt all things with these people were odd these days. As she stood there the tension was so thick a knife wouldn't have been able to cut through it.

Derrik shifted nervously and asked, "Can you come back in a few minutes, I need to talk to Scott?"

Jory replied tactfully, but pointed, "No problem."

Within ten minutes, Derrik gave Jory the financials in a sealed manila envelope. Jory decided to leave and track down Mason. After the meeting, Mason had put in extremely long hours and would be ready to call it a day. They still had two hours to drive home to Manhattan and the sky was taking on an attitude, proving to have a power of its own. They packed everything up that was needed and transportable to use at the Manhattan office. As Jory was leaving Matt's CPA firm, Jory poked her head into Susan's office to tell her goodnight. Susan, too, was startled. Jory noticed Susan was decked out to the hilt in a black velvet and satin evening gown, although an elegant dress, it appeared to be at least one size to small, perhaps two. "You look nice tonight, big plans?"

Susan hesitantly replied, "No!"

That was it, another awkward moment. "No!" with endless minutes of quiet.

Geez, these people are so strange, what the hell is going on around here? Jory wondered to herself as she awkwardly exited Susan's office.

Mason was so intense with his machine and preoccupied with the HMO group coming next week to look at one of their purchased machines that he barely had any time for any other thoughts or conversations. The two started out towards Manhattan and the wind was picking up in speed. Wind was an element one learned to respect in Kansas. It could have unbelievable power and force, in a moments notice. The sky was darkening and sending threatening messages. Radio stations were beeping and dinging broadcast warnings for all the storms that were popping up in Kansas.

The drive home usually consisted of work, too. Everything did. Jory was working on several issues, one of which was the financials she had awkwardly acquired from Derrik, including reviewing Matt's financial reports. She was studying the month's financial report and noticed several discrepancies from last month and a major faux pas on "being out of money."

"Didn't I just spend the whole afternoon with Derrik and DII investors to beg for money because the company was supposedly out of money, completely out? What the hell?" Jory gasped.

The financials showed one hundred and sixty thousand dollars in cash. Granted this would go fast, but still there was a little time. "Last time I checked a hundred and sixty thousand dollars wasn't pocket change," she mumbled sarcastically. The amount DII owed RxBot, LLC jumped twenty thousand from last month, but DII didn't borrow any additional money therefore there shouldn't be an entry of advancing more money. Ten thousand for office furniture? "Oh, my god, Susan's been decorating again. But ten thousand? What? Who authorized this?" She was still mumbling. "Eighty thousand in capitalized engineering costs? Did this mean Matt was spending enormous amounts of money on engineering services no one knew about?" Certainly he knew nothing about engineering. There had to be some mistake. Jory was so restless that she asked Mason to let her drive so he could study the financials and see if she was missing something. With an annoying attitude, he agreed, as he knew she wouldn't give it a rest until he looked them over. Tensions were high enough and he knew it would just be easier to handle it.

Jory took over the drive and Mason was as quiet as a church mouse reviewing all the papers. All of the sudden Jory yelled, "Oh, my God! Mason, look, it's a funnel cloud!"

Mason looked up and to the southwest, he intensely was watching the low-hanging, black-tailed cloud. The cloud appeared to be drawn back up into the sky, for the moment. The two were west of Wichita a few miles and there weren't any ditches, overpasses, off roads or anything to pull over. The interstate was like a maze with the number of orange barrels popping up from the ongoing construction. The tornado changed its mind and in a split second decided to regenerate and come right toward them.

Jory terrified, heart pounding, breathing shallow, yelled, "Mason, what should I do, should we pull over?" Never hesitating, she picked up speed.

"Go, Go, Go," Mason yelled.

Subconsciously, she was wondering where the hell that easygoing guy went—the one that never showed any fear. She desperately needed him back. The gray swirling cloud was about one-half mile away at this time still heading toward the speeding Trooper. Jory glanced down briefly and noticed the speedometer read ninety-five miles per hour. The color of the "great outdoors" turned a sickly, jaundiced, yellowish-brown.

Mason and Jory were both yelling, "Go, Go, Go," and watching so intensely that both were intrigued, scared, and uncertain of every move. They saw the dirt start swirling on the ground in the field next to them and it was even with them.

Mason continued to yell, "Keep going," as the dirt met up with the cloud.

Pounding rain began to hit the windshield.

"Were on the back side of it, the rain is on the backside," Mason explained.

Jory briefly remembered from grade school days that she had learned that about tornadoes, too. At the moment, she wasn't sure if she could put complete faith in this theory. The rain was pounding with such force that the vibration could be felt in her chest and through it a huge orange ball appeared. It was out of proportion to the sky and it dominated and demanded all sight. It was the sun and it was all that remained for the moment. It was so intense it was causing a reflection from the rain on the interstate that decreased the visibility to zero. It reminded her of an eye exam she had once had where the physician shone an intensely bright light into her eye that caused a sort of pain, a pain of torture. Mason watched the back for the tornado and noticed a rainbow that covered the whole sky. It was incredible. There it was again, that ancient promise that never failed to appear. At that moment, they were experiencing every element of weather Kansas had to offer. If Toto would have been in the car, a scene from the "Wizard of Oz" could have been filmed. Jory suddenly worried about her "Toto," Hobbes, but remembered he was in the house and was much safer than she or Mason. The dog had a life, that was for sure. Mason and Jory had lived most of their lives in Kansas and hadn't ever experienced a tornado until now on the unprotected interstate without a place to pull over to seek shelter. By this time it was hailing and the interstate had narrowed to one lane for construction. A semi tractor-trailer was coming in the opposite direction splashing a wave of water directly into the windshield of the stormed Trooper. Jory lost all visibility and was literally driving blindly. Reflexes made her brake, realizing someone would probably end up in her back seat, but all of the sudden she noticed no one was around. Where was everyone? She suddenly hoped she hadn't missed rapture since the setting was obviously an act of God. They must have found some place to pull over, but where?

Mason joked, "They just couldn't keep up with you, Flash!"

The sky continued to be ominous the remainder of the trip. Black clouds with tails, humongous thunderheads revealing their own threat. The white bubbly clouds had a green tint, indicating hail was nearby. The sky was unveiling its form of powerful entertainment from horrific light shows provided by the lightening, to bubbled, textured clouds to a magnitude of colors from multiple rainbows. This had been a true experience. Mason joked with Jory because she had been referred to as Mason's weather nerd. Jory loved weather. She was talking a mile a minute displaying the effect of adrenaline and caffeine, when she realized the danger was over.

She looked at Mason with one of her smiles and said, "Wow, you want to do that again? Do you remember our conversation about what to do if we ever get caught in a tornado? If you recall the number one lesson is to make sure you don't try to outrun it!" She laughed.

Mason had explained the theory that one should always go perpendicular to the tornado? This used to be a joke between the two of them. Even though both of them knew what it meant, they always had different perspectives—as with most scientific topics discussed between the two of them. Jory used to say, if the tornado was big enough and approached as a huge wall cloud, coming directly in front of the vehicle, then going directly into it *would* be perpendicular and she wasn't going to do that.

Mason would roll his eyes and shake his head and say, "You go ahead and go your perpendicular, but leave me the keys!"

When they were safe, Jory smarted off and said, "Mason, I know what it means to go perpendicular!"

It was pretty sad, but the tornado had actually been the highpoint of the day. Subconsciously, they both knew this was the beginning symbolism of their days to come.

KIDDO

The minute the Grays' returned home, and after a few minutes of a very welcomed return from Hobbes, Jory called Derrik. She needed an explanation on the monthly financial report and didn't want to wait a minute longer. Derrik was out for the moment. She left a message, "Derrik, call me. I don't understand most of the figures for this month's financial statement. I'll be up late so please call me back." After a few minutes, the phone rang. Jory answered.

On the other end was a brutally familiar voice, "I hear you are questioning my financial report?" It was Matt. "You are not to discuss these financials with anyone but me!"

Jory becoming very suspicious, just of this statement alone, finds herself wandering the direction of all of this, but remained calm and quiet. "Jory, I haven't the time to make any changes to my financials!"

Jory confidently instructed Matt, "I would like to have DII's accountant, Maddie look at these financials, since I need some help with your explanations."

Inflamed, Matt replied, "Are you accusing me of something Jory?"

"No, Matt, I have to be able to explain these figures to DII and right now, there are several entries I am having trouble understanding. There have been changes since last month, without any authority to change these entries as our contract states or any documentation of actual services rendered for some of the entries."

After several minutes of heated discussion, Matt jolted out of nowhere, "Well, kiddo…"

Jory interrupted and rudely asked, "Matt! Don't call me *kiddo!*"

"Well, kiddo, I will fix these as you want. You don't understand my accounting!" Matt grumbled.

Jory asked, "Is this what creative accounting is?"

Jory, not expecting an affirmation, heard Matt say, "Yes."

Even more confused, Jory continued to listen to Matt ramble forcefully about how he would change the royalties and the loans to what they previously were, but no more money would be loaned to DII. He continued to ramble that there was a discrepancy in one of the note forms that was suppose to be fifteen thousand, not fifty thousand.

Jory, thought to herself, *What an incompetent son-of-a-bitch! What accountant makes a mistake like that when it was originally agreed upon to be fifty thousand dollars? What was he doing, or trying to do?*

Bickering continued on and on with Matt doing most of it. Jory could not get one word in. One of Jory's learned talents from pharmacy school was to let angry people vent. When they finished, then, and only then, was a reply appropriate. Finally, after letting Matt go on and on, the conversation ended. Matt agreed to fix the financials to match actual transactions. *Now that's a novel idea*, Jory thought. There was a strange noise interrupting the conversation, a beep of some sort. All of the time Jory was talking, she felt as if someone was listening in, but wrote it off as being paranoid. *Matt's paranoia must be rubbing off on me*, she thought to herself.

When the beeps were finished Matt replied, "That was my keyboard." Subconsciously, that beep was familiar to Jory. It wasn't from a keyboard, but she was totally preoccupied with the details at hand that she didn't have the energy or time to place it. Jory hung up very unsettled. She had a feeling of doom.

SOCKS AND PARKING PLACES

Matt had pointed out upon numerous occasions that he would be the only one on the signature card for the RxBot, LLC accounts. Since he was the accountant, he needed to be the one. Jory had inquired about this issue several times, mainly for the concern if something happened to him, it would be wise to have another name on the signature card for protection. This was unheard of to Matt. During a heated conversation this issue came up and Matt said Derrik was on the signature card. Derrik had told Jory at the meeting that afternoon that he wasn't even on it. When Jory confronted Matt about adding another partner to the card, Matt told Jory she could not be on it. Jory wanted to scream, but forced herself to keep her composure and replied, "Matt, not me, but what about Mason?"

Matt divertingly replied, "He didn't ask." Another untruth.

Jory could think of three times it had been brought up by Mason when she was around. She knew anything she brought up financially was pretty much a moot point with Matt. After all, he knew all and no one was going to tell him or get anything from him, unless he wanted it that way.

After hanging up, Jory and Mason discussed the conversation for hours. Both of them knew there was something horribly wrong, but neither wanted to confront it. The HMO was coming in a week and Mason had to be totally ready for the presentation and this took all his energy. Derrik had assured Mason that if he couldn't get the machine ready in time he would call the HMO and cancel the showing. Mason was killing himself trying to get the machine back to being demonstrable, but now both he and Jory were exhausted and it was time for bed. Another night of tossing and turning.

Mistakenly taking the ringing of the phone for the alarm at six thirty the next morning, Jory awakened and for a brief second oriented herself to answer the phone. Mason had already left for Wichita at five. Jory sleepily answered and heard that voice no one would want to wake up to. It was Matt. She thought she was having a nightmare of last night and he was still going off on her. Matt was obsessing over the signature card issue, of all things. After all, Matt was the master of obsessing. Jory just wanted the financials to be correct and now the main issue with Matt seemed to be the signature card. There could be no bigger red flag than this, but what was he doing? Was it just his paranoia? One could never be sure what the obsession issue would be for the day. Matt stated, "Jory, it is essential I keep total control over the bank accounts, no one else needs to be writing checks."

"No one wants to write checks, Matt. Another person on the signature card was for protection," Jory reiterated.

"No," Matt interrupted. "Ya know, Jory, you and Mason have access on-line to all the financials through my computer system. You always have had access."

Jory, wondering what he was up to, asked, "How come you never told us that before now?" (Knowing he just added this lovely new feature to their benefits package of being RxBot, LLC, especially since he made the point of "always" having access).

"You never asked. Just log in and look at it." Matt suggested. This was totally out of character unless there was something Matt was going to have unveiled on his terms.

"Matt, I have to get to work. We will have to continue this conversation later!" Jory concluded.

Matt, having to get in the last word, asked, "What about the user manuals? Are you done yet, kiddo?"

Jory laughed. "You're kidding right?" She knew if he had any technological intellect they wouldn't be having this conversation. "Besides, since it is an ongoing project it was just decided two weeks ago that I would be doing it. Goodbye, Matt."

Jory was getting ready to walk out the door, on her way to work, when she heard the fax machine take off for another busy day.

Revised Financial Statement, per our Discussion —Matt

Jory, completely confused, briefly studied the financials and, sure enough, everything was exactly as requested. "What? He just changes and moves entries at his own whim? God, please don't let this be what it appears to be," she muttered.

Two days, just two until the showing of this whole modified RxBot to the HMO. Mason knew he couldn't do it. He was feeling like the fall guy. Even though Derrik gave him the right to cancel the showing he still felt queasy and uneasy. He told Derrik to cancel and Derrik said they still had time to "keep on trying." Mason was starting to take on the idea that perhaps they wanted the demonstration to fail because they didn't want to honor the contract from the beginning with the HMO. The HMO was an original, DII, interested customer. They had gotten a good price since they were eager to be patient and take somewhat of a risk. Matt wanted to charge them a higher price and hated the original contract. Mason was starting to feel sick physically from all the work and all the manipulating that was going on. It was becoming hard to see what was really going on. He worked continuously around the clock for the entire week and only slept when it became a necessity. He was extremely dedicated, but knew this wasn't going to happen like it needed to. He just knew it. He had shown the machine a million times before. With the new changes, software changes, and all of Matt's changes, RxBot was not working correctly. Matt's changes were throwing many aspects of the whole machine off. It just wasn't ready for a demonstration. The night before the scheduled showing, he went home and was beside himself with this dilemma. Jory wasn't much better. They took a walk in the park to try to clear their minds. One thing led to another and Jory ended up begging Mason not to go through with the showing, if he felt it would turn out so poorly. "Wouldn't it be better to cancel than to have a bad showing?" she asked Mason. They ended up getting into a heated argument and the yelling and screaming began. Jory had lost trust in Matt and Derrik and felt certain they wanted to lose the HMO account. Mason was feeling like the "fall guy". If the showing went poorly, it was his fault, if it didn't take place, it was his fault. It just wasn't ready to be shown yet with Matt making changes. At that moment, it was in one of the biggest messes it had been in—in quite some time. Truth be known, it was closer to being ready to show to customers a few months earlier. The walk seemed longer than usual and not near as enjoyable. When they reached "dead dog hill" Jory was so upset she couldn't breath, not from the hill, but from the anguish of it all. She asked Mason again not to do the demo if it was going to fail. There was too much at stake. By the end of the walk, Mason had made his decision to cancel the demonstration. He would go home, call Derrik, and instruct him to cancel. It was short notice, but it could still be done without too much harm. Some of course, but damage control would save the contract. This was the agreement from the very beginning and Mason had been trying to tell Derrik and Matt over and over it wasn't ready. Mason made the phone call. Derrik wasn't happy, but agreed to call the HMO and reschedule the viewing of RxBot. "All right, not that much harm done," Mason convinced himself. Mason had decided to stay at DII the next day. He tried to get caught up on some of the Manhattan duties that had been extremely neglected lately plus he needed a break from these CPA's!

The morning of the scheduled showing, Derrik called last minute and told Mason he had to be in Wichita in two hours to show the machine to the HMO because he decided to "not" cancel or reschedule the demonstration of RxBot. Mason was livid and told Derrik there was no way he could make it and he knew Derrik knew that.

"What are you doing Derrik? You said you would reschedule it!"

"It's just too late!" Derrik moaned.

"You want to talk "too late" Derrik, two hours to get ready, how convenient for you and Matt that I can't make it in two hours. Call them back, now and cancel that showing, Derrik!" Mason demanded.

Matt's paranoia was rubbing off on Derrik because before they hung up Derrik puzzlingly asked, "You're developing something else without us, aren't you?"

Mason was dumbfounded and almost refused to answer, but he found himself asking, "What the hell are you talking about, Derrik. I am doing everything humanly possible to see this creation get on the market with absolutely no help from you guys, only obstacles from you two. It's as if you don't want us to succeed. Is that right, Derrik?"

There was no answer.

YES MAN

Over the months it had become apparent that Derrik's character was severely flawed. The tall, stringiness of the man only helped prove he must have been the whiny classroom wimp as a child. He was that "wimpy" bully who lied and stole from everyone, but never took the blame. The "uh-uh, wasn't my fault" kid. He was the scrawny, freckled-faced troublemaker that pulled the pigtails of the little red-headed girls. As an adult, he wasn't an intelligent man, just larger than his youth, but he still carried with him these same attributes. He wasn't a competent man and most of all he wasn't a good man. He always prided himself for being slick and had found early on in life that if he said everything just like people wanted to hear he could get away with anything. He had no qualms about doing anything, signing anything, as he knew he could always squirm like a slithering snake right out of the situation. It had always worked for him to this point. He bragged, upon numerous occasions about this attribute.

Derrik had a family that was fully in the dark over Derrik's operations. Derrik loved the appearance his family life gave him. It was debatable whether Derrik was capable of feeling any emotion, other than greed. Derrik being a "robot" responded point to point to every command, a transparent figure of a father, a programmed CPA. Every move Derrik made was mapped out for him and programmed by someone else. When Derrik started his first job as a CPA, his firm suggested what church he and his family should attend. And of course, he then attended that particular church. Derrik figured he might as well please his boss and get as far as he could from the very start. If his boss said, "Jump," then he jumped. If they said, "Steal," he would steal, whatever it took. Without any additional thinking, this logic carried him through for many, many years. Derrik had a wife, and two adopted children. The adopted children added to that "fine figure of a father" image he loved to portray. To many and especially Matt, Derrik was borderline on his abilities to follow through successfully on any commands, but he was as loyal to Matt as Matt could find. Matt and Derrik blamed each other for any inferior qualities that surfaced, in any situation. Both were inadequate at inventing or developing anything, but both could follow a flow-charted plan, and steal. Any deviation from the plan and trouble could sit in. Their egos alone or added together were so large that to a keen observer it could appear to be a pathological disorder. As Derrik had mentioned at one of the first meetings, Matt truly did have some medical disorders. It was becoming obvious.

DEMO

While Mason was trying to work at DII, Nathan called to tell Mason that the HMO had arrived and that they were all supposed to meet at the demo. What should he do? Nathan was told that Mason had called earlier and that he and Jory would not be making it to the demo. He was told something came up that needed taken care of as soon as possible. Mason couldn't believe it. All his efforts and dreams sidestepped by these two idiots. He was extremely upset and couldn't think straight. His face was hot with anger. He was devastated. What could this all possibly mean? He knew Nathan's loyalties were with him. He told him to ride it out and to keep him posted as to what transpired over the day. No one was sure that Derrik or Matt could even run RxBot to demonstrate it. Locating the "on" button was above their technical abilities. Mason and Nathan knew they would put Nathan in an awkward position and make him responsible for that effort. The demo was made very short to show only what was working and to avoid any clumsy mistakes made by Matt or Derrik. It took all of five minutes without too many disasters other than these people traveled from Washington to see five minutes of their machine and basically saw turning it on and off.

The extremely long day finally drew into evening when Nathan was asked, "What is going on with Mason and Jory?"

Matt was inquisitive and assuming with his questioning. He asked Nathan if Mason and Jory were having health or marital problems that would lead them to such drastic measures as to not show up for the demonstration. Of course, Matt didn't mention that they only gave Mason two hours notice to show up for the demonstration, after they had informed him the showing would be cancelled. Mason was sure Matt figured he could win Nathan over. He would try by any means, most for sure, not morally fit. If he had too, he would "buy" him. He continued to tell Nathan how weird it was, especially since the machine was so close to being a success. It was puzzling as to why Mason would want to "bail" now. Who would ever believe an inventor of something of this magnitude would "bail" and with it proving to be successful? Only the insane.

DESPERATE MEASURES FOR DESPERATE TIMES

It was finally the weekend. Weekends used to be "weekends!" The long awaited vacation of the week. They were the big sigh that followed the extremely stressful weeks. Both Mason and Jory tried to still think of weekends as, "time off." Lately, all the weekends, all the weeks, all the days, all the long hours were spent in Wichita, designing, building, manufacturing Mason's machine. Theoretically, it was time to breath, at least somewhat. Everyone was stressed to the hilt. Mason and Jory played every scenario over and over in their heads giving everyone involved, the benefit of the doubt. They tried to blame discrepancies on exhaustion and paranoia. Saturday night, after talking about every possible explanation, Mason decided to log into the LLC financial reports, as Matt had suggested. Matt had supposedly left town for a couple of days, unexplained, as he often did.

Login, Mason typed, *RxBot*. Next the word, "password", appeared on the screen, Mason typed *success*. To pull up the financial information he then logged into the accounting software with the provided user name and password. He got on without incident, but didn't like or understand what he saw. Mason logged off. They both pondered on what their next step should be. It was decided to look at the financials again. He and Jory sat still, listening, and watching the screen to pop up to allow him access. After a few seconds, the screen popped up an *ACCESS DENIED* message. Matt was on the other end, locking Mason out of the accounting software. Mason looked for a work around. Scanning the directories, he found the RxBot directory.

"Oh, my God!" he whispered.

Jory sat back, listening and watching, not saying a word. It was one of those moments that neither one wanted to end or to go forward. Mase knew that his next actions would be toeing the line, but he knew he had to do it. He could download all the financial data files and email them to Maddie. She had the same software, which would allow her to access the files and then print the financial reports. His gut feeling now superseded the logic he normally used. His mind and hands were shaking and moving so swiftly that it overshadowed him to actually evaluate his actions. It took an hour to download everything. After the download was completed, Mason printed the information. Files he didn't even know existed and all named in some manner for "Matt Coggins..." The paper raced out of the printer, as if the printer knowingly couldn't print fast enough. It was as if it was trying to give a hand to Mason and Jory. Mason and Jory were sitting in complete silence while waiting for all the dreaded results. Jory was holding her head in her sweaty hands. They both knew the situation was getting serious for them to be doing what they were doing. No longer could they allow giving anyone the benefit of the doubt. It was desperate measures for desperate times.

Finally, the printer stopped, the papers were all upside down. Hesitantly, Mason grabbed the stack of paper and for that one second that seemed like an eternity, Mason and Jory glanced at each other. A million thoughts raced through each of their minds. Innocence and trust were no longer valid attributes for them to use. Both of them knew the results of the stacks of paper, contained answers they may not want to know.

Both of them were sitting on the floor in Mason's cluttered office. In the past, many times Jory joked with Mason about the cluttered room—never understanding how he could find a single thing. Mason would refer to two signs he kept in his room to validate his organizational skills. One read "Einstein's desk was messy too" and the other, "A cluttered desk is a sign of a creative mind." She'd snicker; sometimes from the amusement, but other times she was slightly frustrated with this enterpriser's room since she, after all, was the symmetrical one. Mason flipped over the financials and both of them scanned the first page so quickly as if both had just completed an Evelyn Wood speed-reading class.

Mason, red-faced and sweating, yelled, "God Damn, those son-of-a-bitches!!! God, no!!"

Jory, shaken, asked, "Mason, what? What is this? No, Oh my God, No!" She felt herself weaken, thinking she may actually faint.

The financials for the last four months read:

> $150,000.00 to Matt Coggins for capitalized engineering costs, computer hardware, office furniture, and office expenses.
> $100,000.00 to Matt Coggins for his "related companies"
> $50,000.00 to Matt Coggins for utilities and accounting services.
> $20,000.00 to Susan Coggins for her company "Horse supplies."
> $75,000.00 to Matt Coggins for rent, software development.
> $100,000.00 to Derrik Peters for related services.

And the list went on and on and on with names and amounts that Mason and Jory had never heard of, obviously. Every item went to one of the three white collar, criminal CPAs.

Jory without thinking, jumped up, trembling, ran to the door and bolted all the locks. Without noticing, she was on the line waiting for Maddie.

Hours and hours had passed. Discussions, explanations, confirmations and faxes continued endlessly throughout the night with Maddie. Maddie was extremely intelligent and had become a friend one could only hope for. It was just a "beni" that she was family, too. She was extremely trustworthy. Mason and Jory needed her help so badly right now, but hated they had to draw her into this neurotic mess. From the initial examination of the documents she was asking questions about the "related companies."

"Why did the related companies have the same address as Matt's office and why so much money to them? Were payments authorized by anyone other than Matt? Why are there weird titles for entries and not the traditional names? Why are there so many individual payments to people that are not RxBot, LLC employees? Why isn't Matt keeping books on an accrual basis, why isn't there an accounts payable? Why one thousand dollars per month for pager usage? Why so many journals, and not a general journal? This journal issue just makes it harder to follow." There were thirteen journals.

She continued, "Why was Matt's brother-in-law paid for services before RxBot, LLC, agreed to use his expertise? Why wasn't Mason on the signature cards? Why are there accounting charges from other accounting firms? Why is Susan being paid through her horse business? Why? Why? Why?" It was mind-boggling. Neither being an accountant and not understanding all the questions, they definitely understood the direction the questions were leading.

Hours and hours had passed and it was two in the morning and both Mason and Jory were still full of energy from all of the adrenaline of the breaking news. Mason decided to get back on line. His first attempt didn't work. His second attempt didn't work. His third attempt took longer than usual and within several minutes a message "ACCESS DENIED" appeared on the screen.

Mason yelled to Jory, "Jory come here and bring the camcorder. Hurry!" From this point on, Mason and Jory had been locked out of any information about the LLC, about their company and about their invention. They were being forced to bail!

SPECIAL MEETING

June 1, the first day of summer break. Jory's first official day off from the pharmacy, for the entire summer. What a much needed break. Working at the pharmacy part time and working at DII and RxBot, LLC *full* time had become too much. The two o'clock chime was playing its tune and the doorbell rang simultaneously creating an out of tune chorus. Jory energetically ran down the stairs to answer the door. Federal Express was at the door with two envelopes. "Mr. Mason Gray, and Mrs. Jory Gray" from the office of Matt Coggins, CPA. "Sign here please, ma'am," the man said sympathetically.

Did he know? Jory's mind racing, heart racing, hands shaking, she nervously signed for the letters and mumbled a quiet, "Thank you."

Mason was in Wichita, as he always was these days, working on the machine even after acquiring the information about a possible embezzlement over the weekend. He was almost impossible to get a hold of except by his cell phone. Jory found a fraction of a second to realize the disappointment that Matt had interrupted her summer vacation from the pharmacy. It was suppose to be such an exciting summer. The plans were that she would be traveling for RxBot installations all over the world—an opportunity of a lifetime. She tore open the white envelope as fast and violently as she could to dreadfully read:

RXBOT, LLC
NOTICE OF SPECIAL MEETING OF MEMBERS
June 1, 2004
TO OUR MEMBERS:
Notice is hereby given that a special meeting of members of RxBot, L.L.C. (hereinafter called the "Company") will be held at the offices of the Company, Wichita, Kansas at 9:00 o'clock **a.**m., central standard time, the 14th day of June, 2004, for the following purposes:
1. To appoint Matt E. Coggins to act as Chairman of the meeting and Derrik W. Peters to act as secretary of the meeting.
2. To consider and vote upon the expulsion of Mason L Gray, Jory M. Gray and John E. Crowe as members of the Company.
3. To consider and vote upon the removal of Mason L. Gray from the office of President of the company.
4. To consider and vote upon the removal of Jory M. Gray as Director of Pharmacy operations of the Company.
5. To consider and vote upon the removal of Mason L. Gray as a manager of the Company.
6. To consider and vote upon the termination of the employment of Mason L. Gray as an employee of the Company.
7. To consider and vote upon the termination of the employment of Jory M. Gray as an employee of the Company.
8. To consider and vote upon the adoption of a resolution providing that in the event the Company continues after the expulsion of a member, then the expelled member shall be deemed a permitted transferee and as such shall not be

entitled to participate in any manner in the management of the Company's affairs, vote, receive any information of Company transactions or inspect the Company books. The expelled member shall merely be entitled to receive, in accordance with the operating Agreement of the Company, the share of profits or other compensation by way of income and the return of contributions to which the expelled member would be entitled had he or she not been expelled.
9. To transact such other business as may properly be brought before the meeting.
Any member, present at the meeting by proxy, may, upon request, participate in the meeting by means of conference telephone; provided that such member's proxy shall vote, according to the number of votes which such member would have been entitled to cast and with all the powers which such member would be entitled to exercise if personally present and such participation in the meeting.
RXBOT, LLC
By request of the following four (4) members:
Matt Coggins
Derrik W. Peters
Jack Wilson
Oscar Tyler

"Oh my God! No!! Oh my God." Tears filled Jory's eyes, her hands trembled, fear and weakness spread to her entire body as she ran upstairs and frantically dialed Mason's cell phone, only to hear the "out of range" message. Tears falling and following one after another, to the point she couldn't keep up to dry them, she dialed the only number she had a remote chance of reaching Mason on any given day. Listening to quivering telephone tones she whispered frantically, "Please God, please, let him be there, please dear God." She had dialed MDT manufacturing where

Mason had spent endless hours overlooking the assembly of his creation.

"Hello," she heard.

With incredible relief she spewed out, "Mason, thank God you are there."

"What's wrong?" Mason worriedly asked.

Jory could hardly breathe and with hesitation told Mason, "Mason, they are throwing us out, taking our company. We both received notice." Dead silence took over.

After hanging up, dazed, Mason was experiencing the same symptoms Jory had experienced, but he was overtaken with anger and confusion. After he pondered over the news for thirty minutes he raced over to Matt's office and confronted Matt and Derrik. He had been waiting until Matt and Derrik would be together to confront them about the financial information Mason had downloaded.

He entered the house that led to Matt's office and heard the chatter of the staff. Silence enveloped the air when Mason appeared. "What's going on, Matt?"

Matt, unaware that Mason received the news, answered, "Received the vial handler motors?"

Mason interrupted, "Matt, Jory told me about the letter we both received today."

Matt, dismissing the urgency, replied, "It's just a meeting to discuss the future of the company."

"Just a meeting to discuss the future of the company?" Mason repeated in an agitated state. "I'd say that is a pretty damn big meeting, what's really going on, Matt?"

Matt totally dismissed Mason and, as he was walking away, he muttered, "We'll discuss all of this at the meeting, I am too busy to be bothered right now."

"Too busy not being involved in daily activities of RxBot, Matt?" Mason sarcastically asked. Mason knowingly observing it futile to try and discuss anything with Matt, changed directions and went to find Derrik. As he entered Derrik's office, Derrik acted as if nothing had changed and was all smiles and jollies, but had a slightly red face.

Mason immediately exposed his purpose "Derrik, what the hell are you doing? Why are you doing this?"

Derrik kept his mousy smile, face now turning beat red, and repeated, "It is just a meeting." He was obviously repeating a rehearsed statement Matt had provided.

"Derrik, you know Matt will turn on you, too, and you better decide now what side of the fence you are on because I will **never** let this happen. Never. If you cross that line there won't be any going back. Don't make the biggest mistake of your life!" At that point, Mason was unaware that Derrik Peters had already made his biggest mistakes in life.

As Mason was getting ready to leave he heard Derrik repeat what he was programmed to repeat, "It is just a meeting to decide the future of the company, Mason."

In Mason's mind he wondered if the man could ever think or speak for himself. Doom hanging from every molecule of air, with the entire staff, silent as mice and motionless as mannequins, Mason left abruptly and harshly and went back to MDT manufacturing. He felt sick. He entered the large metal doors to find Gus Dobbs sitting at his desk, white as a sheet. Mason could tell something was wrong and asked, "Gus, can I talk to you? I need to get my things out of here."

Gus explained, "Mason, in order for me to keep the contract for RxBot, I have been warned not to let you leave with anything. If I do not use all of Coggins accounting services he will see that RxBot goes somewhere else which I can't afford at this time." Matt had used his position with the LLC to force MDT to purchase goods and services from his CPA firm. This allowed Matt to personally benefit and seriously jeopardize the LLC's relationship with the supplier.

Mason confusingly replied, "The problem with that, Gus, is that RxBot is my product and I have controlling interest in the company so the threat is idle."

Gus now more confused and even paler than before, although that seemed impossible, replied, "That is what Matt said you would say and now I don't know where I stand, but until I do, I am not willing to make any rash decisions or to release anything."

Mason in a total state of confusion and despair turned around and left. The drive home was taken up with preoccupation of the day. Before he knew it, he was home and for some reason for the first time in his life he looked up at his warm, quaint limestone home and hesitated to walk through the front door. He didn't want to enter the uncertain future that lied ahead. He had no choice, but to cross that threshold and deal with the darkness of this reality in fighting for his company, his invention and perhaps the fight in keeping his life.

Jory was impatiently waiting for his arrival. When he opened the front door she was right there. They threw their arms around each other and both were talking a mile a minute. The only difference was Mason's face was red with anger and Jory had tears running down her cheeks.

OPTIONS

After calming down somewhat, the two of them sat on the couch and read the "Special Meeting" notice close to a million times. It was late, but there had to be some way to catch Jack Livingston (the new, cheaper, appointed, DII attorney) and get some legal advice. Fortunately, they did just that and called an "after hours" number and were able to talk with him. Explaining the notice and reading it several times, Jack had Mason pull out several documents to make sure everything was in place to "not" let this happen. One of the documents Jack immediately had Mason pull was the Operating Agreement that had been signed by Matt, Derrik, John, Oscar and Mason. All documents had been reviewed, adjusted, reviewed and reviewed to the point of acquiring much expense. It was amazing that Jack Livingston and Phil Kalivoda had helped form the LLC, but now there seemed to be some doubt in Jack's voice that was very unsettling. Jack mentioned an attorney's name that should probably get involved in this. Rick Houser. He was better at these "types of cases."

Jory, fuming, was overcome with emotion, and wondering, *What the hell does he mean THIS TYPE OF CASE?* "We are a case?" she screamed. "Oh my God!"

Mason's hand was scribbling down Rick Houser's number as he held up one hand to quiet Jory. The look he gave her probably would have been enough to do the job, but added the hand gesture to make sure she got the point. Jack assured Mason that he would arrange a conversation to be taken place that night.

After forty-five minutes of hashing over documents with Rick Houser, he needed a few minutes and wanted them faxed to him. All this was done on the phone and occupied most of the evening trying to find a way to salvage their positions, their company, their invention and their future. The only thing that Mason could find was a clause that stated, "If one manager resigned the whole structure would be dissolved." So this was it—the *only* choice.

Rick agreed with Mason that this was his "only" choice. Rick said to "sleep on it" and that he would need a fifteen thousand dollar retainer for him to continue. Jory was furious. Fifteen thousand to retain him for what, so Mason could resolve this mess? That is what happened so far. Mason found the clause, not the experienced attorney. This was almost too much to digest for one evening. Putting their faith and lives in the hands of a complete stranger, an attorney, wasn't very comforting. Why would he care about their future except to gain the fifteen thousand dollars? Fifteen thousand was the absolute most the Grays could do and it was a complete stretch. This was the last of their life savings, the absolute last of it and an additional cash advance off of one of the several credit cards they had been using to sustain DII. To most, it probably didn't seem like much, but to them it was earned the old fashioned way and it was blood, sweat, and tears. How ironic since that was what it was going to be used for.

Mason and Jory had slept on their one and only option. Both wondered how come there was only one lame one at that. One measly option in the agreement, which the attorneys had written when the LLC was formed—so much for trusting attorneys to keep one out of trouble. Attorneys had created this mess. They were involved from day one to protect the company and RxBot from this very thing happening. Mason had been talking with John Crowe and in everyone's best interest it was decided that John would resign as a member of the LLC to dissolve the LLC. It was really the only choice in the resignation of a member due to the Gray's being so intimately involved. The Grays and John Crowe would lose all of their investment if they didn't take immediate action. John was such an incredible man and trusted Mason on this issue of resigning. He took the resignation and knew it was what he had to do.

The next day, Jory found herself rearranging everything in the house, cleaning out closets, drawers, having her hair cut, changing everything as if it would make some sort of difference. She had to do something with all of her nervous energy. She had been a swimmer since college and swam routinely. When times would get stressful she would resort to even more swimming. Her walks and her swims helped her keep her sanity.

Once Rick was told of their decision to have John Crowe resign and dissolve the LLC, the fifteen thousand dollars was sent. The money got the gears in motion. John Crowe had a lifelong friend that was an attorney and he had decided to retain him for himself. An army of attorneys was starting to look like what it was going to take. He felt this would strengthen the case. A restraining order put on the LLC was the plan to keep any meeting from being held on the expulsion of the Gray's or any other meeting, for that matter. As soon as the paper work could be typed up, Matt, Derrick, Oscar and Jack would all receive notice. In the mean time, Rick told Mason to try and talk to Matt and see if there would be any way to resolve this matter other than in court. Rick suggested that Mason try to buy out Matt and Derrik, and to try anything to get them out of the LLC so Mason could continue the success of his invention.

Mason continued to work at DII and hopefully the daily routine would in the end be profitable and worthwhile to both companies. Mason spent most of the day on the telephone to attorneys and anyone he could think of that might be able to help. In between the numerous phone calls Mason decided to call Matt. He had to. He wouldn't accuse him of anything, but try one last time to settle this before it got out of hand or in the hands of the courts.

As Mason listened to the phone line delivering the ring to Matt his mind raced to find the right words.

His thoughts were interrupted with RxBot, LLC. "This is Angela, may I help you?"

Matt came on the phone, "Okay, Mason, can you hear me?"

Mason replied, "Sure."

Matt again replied, "Okay."

Mason started, "Well, I have been thinking through this and I guess there's no point in beating around the bush or delaying it. I think it would be in the best interest of the company and allow us to move forward if you step out of this organization in lieu of what has transpired recently."

Matt responded, "Uh-uh—which company are we talking about?"

Mason confusingly replied, "Well the…"

Matt interrupted, "RxBot or which company are we talking about this being in the best interest of…"

Mason, again confused, "Of the LLC!" He was thinking, *What an idiot.*

Matt stated finally, "Of RxBot, okay, so you want me to step out of RxBot, LLC?"

Mason was wondering if this guy was drugged or what, in the way he was repeating absolutely everything and not making any sense…Mason figured he must be writing everything down or recording the conversation… "Matt, that's the only company we are involved in that I know of."

Matt again spoke, "Well, you said in the best interest of the company, so I just wanted to—you're saying this would be in the best interest of RxBot?"

Mason angrily and louder answered, "Yeeessss, Matt." Mason was losing his patience, which was pretty limited these days anyway. Crime and deceit had obviously robbed Matt of his brain.

Matt, now confirming Mason's suspicions… "Okay, step out of

the LLC. I'm just making some notes here as we talk."

Mason responded, "Okay."

Matt continued, "All right, well, that's a proposal that could be made, and I suppose to be considered——certainly to be considered. What's— you don't need to explain the reason to me for it. I'm not surprised that you feel that way 'cause you and I have not been getting along that well lately on some of these issues, and I had indicated when you were up here the other day that I just didn't feel there was a basis of trust or a very good working relationship, so other than me stepping out, who's going to step in and who's going to run the company? In other words, what would the next move be?"

Mason, trying to offer suggestions, said, "Well, I think it's important to get this passed first because I think this is a major issue for us. How we move forward isn't certain until we decide on whether we can move past this issue or not."

Matt responded, "So, in other words, you'd like me to step out and then decide what to do from there. How do you propose to have me step out? You mean, like resign, or be bought out or what do you have in mind?"

Mason subconsciously thinking, *My boot on your ass would be the simplest way...!* He continued, "Well, I think it would be best if you were out completely. Whether we buy you out or whatever we can work out."

Matt listening offers, asked, "Do you have any specifics in mind there?"

Mason thought, *Oh, brother, how long is he going to stretch this conversation out? Okay, Mase, just keep your composure.* "No, I don't!" *Ooooh, that was lame, but I can't lose it here,* he thought.

Matt, still with him, added, "Well, you know what, if we were able to have meetings without being impeded by the court then these kinds of things could be discussed, considered, and voted on."

Mason, still composed and trying, said, "Yeah, well, I think we've tried that. When I came over to talk to you—you indicated there was nothing to discuss and we felt we had to protect ourselves. If you'd like to meet and discuss how we resolve this, we would be glad to meet and do that."

Matt continued, "Mason, the reason I said there was nothing to discuss was because we've discussed things before and found out that agreements that were made were not kept and probably the most flagrant of these relates to the advancing of funds on advanced royalties and also to the confidentiality agreement and I just—— what's the point in discussing when there isn't any follow through. It's just talk at this point."

Mason, knowingly putting a burr under Matt's ass, said, "Let's just fill the room with attorneys and we'll get it all down on paper and make it happen."

Matt interruped, "The reason that we went through the expulsion proceedings...we didn't go through them...the reason that we proposed that they be considered was because we felt you were working against the best interest in the LLC, watching out for DII and having that 'conflict of interest.' Everyone at this end feels it would be in the best interest of the LLC to have you, Jory and John out and let me run things, but now you have orchestrated a plan to terminate the company."

Mason had to bite his tongue to NOT say, *What company are we talking about?* He then continued, "Well, I was protecting my interest as well as the interests of the other members."

Matt answered in a very loud voice, "Well, how do you say that you're protecting your interest when you've contacted John Crow and had him resign so that you and Jory could then fail to consent and dissolve the company and cause the company to lose its primary asset, which is a license? How can you say that's in the best interest of the company?"

Mason confidently added, "Well, it is in the best interest of the company."

"For it to be dissolved and lose its license? It may be in your best interest and Jory's and John's, but it's not in the best interest of RxBot, LLC, for it to lose its license and go out of business, is it?" Matt asked.

"Well, I think this is something that looks like we'll end up settling in the courts. Matt, 'cause I can tell you're not interested in cooperating on this. So, I was hoping that we might be able to come to some resolution on this and be able to move it forward, but it doesn't look like you're interested in doing that. I have been and am doing everything I know humanly possible to protect the interest of the members of the LLC," Mason tried to explain.

"If this were true then you should agree to let us have the meeting to decide who should be running this company," Matt said.

"Forget it Matt, there is obviously no resolution to be made today. Do you have anything else you want to discuss?" was Mason's final request.

"Oh yeah, plenty, but I suppose you would require attorneys to be here," Matt responded.

"That's right!" Mason answered with finality.

Matt, giving up, said, "Well, I can't think of anything else to talk about then."

Mason, seeing no resolution, replied, "All right then."

The next week was a nightmare. The restraining order was going to be fought in local court with Mason and Jory's neighbors acting as counsel for the other side and another neighbor as the judge. This should normally be a good thing, but it was the judicial system so who knew what the rules would be. It worried Jory even more because she thought it could work against them by knowing the attorney and the judge causing it to look like a bias. In the meantime, while waiting, court papers from the Secretary of State's office were delivered to Mason. As he opened the envelope his face turned from his lately acquired ashy gray color to white then red with anger.

"Those son of a bitches, how the hell can they do this?" The forms read that the President and owner of RxBot, LLC had been changed from Mason Gray to Matt Coggins. Mason and Jory were beside themselves and in a state of panic and confusion. Jory called Rick and explained what they had received and begged for an explanation on how something like this could take place.

After hyperventilating with panic and interjecting her "buts, and how's" a million times and turning blue in the face to get Rick to understand where she was coming from Rick finally said, "Jory, take a deep breath, it will all be nullified in court." That statement entered Jory's heart like a long, cold, metal sword. Jory felt as if the sword had actually pierced her heart and the blood had all run from her body. She was coherent, but not hearing.

She found the strength to ask, "What are you talking about NULLIFY IN COURT? What about RIGHT NOW? Rick, you've got to stop this now! How can they walk into the Secretary of State's office and change papers to change companies' ownership's without questions asked? What about justice, what about our legal system?" Jory was mad, really mad, ear burning mad. She now understood rage. Angrily, she said, "This can't be."

Rick eventually calmed Jory down to a mild fury and the conversation ended with her having to accept it as a legal battle and she and Mason were so screwed. It was another really crappy day. Unknowingly that it would end even crappier than the day before—which if told the day before she wouldn't have believed it could get worse. She hated the pattern to what she was seeing here. Rick would be in town for court in a couple of days and they would discuss this further, without a doubt. He told Jory, "Jory, don't worry."

Jory thought, *Yeah, easy for him to say since he just took the last of our life savings and knowing it wasn't his life on the line.* She worried sick about how much Rick would actually be willing to help for a measly fifteen thousand, as an attorney would see it. All of this deceit and betrayal was new to them. Neither Mason nor Jory were equipped with the knowledge to play this game. She had to do something. She went swimming. She was swimming so much lately her shoulders were feeling it. Swimming and her sanity were starting to be proportional which wasn't going to help her shoulders.

COURT—DAY ONE

It must have been a hundred and twenty degrees outside. Mason and Jory sat under an old oak tree at the courthouse in the shade, but both were still dripping wet from the heat of the day. Rick showed up, visited with small meaningless chatter and explained what would happen throughout the day.

Court came and went with the restraining order being put in place. This was a victory for Mason, Jory and their companies. The special meeting to expel Mason, Jory, and John was legally stopped. After the hearing, the judge wanted to visit with Rick for a few minutes. Unknown to all, what the meeting was about, whatever the issue was, it changed Rick somehow.

Matt, being Matt and hating attorneys, had *his* special meeting also and with his "make-believe" hearing, expelled Mason, Jory, and John.

When Jory heard all of this, she thought, Let me guess, it will be nullified in court.

UNFAMILIAR TERRITORY

What now? It was decided that DII investors and attorneys should meet to decide what plan of action should be taken at this point. It would be a serious meeting, a meeting of the minds and of the money. All the major DII investors would meet to discuss all available options.

The meeting was scheduled for the following week, which had now approached late July. It was about one hour before the meeting when Rick decided to tell Mason and Jory he couldn't be their attorney anymore. Obviously, he had used all of the retainer money, which came as no surprise to anyone that had been screwed before. It was becoming apparent that the legal system was not immune to injustice. He was "so kind" as to stay for the meeting, provide counsel and add his two bits. Mason told Rick that if he stayed Mason would not pay him any additional money. Mason made it clear that Rick owed it to him and Jory to stay. Both Mason and Jory waited for Rick to walk away, but he didn't and actually did stay for the entire meeting. As a friendly gesture, he added insult to injury and handed Mason a pound of coffee beans from his trip to Seattle as Rick knew how much Mason enjoyed coffee. Even though Rick saw this as a nice gesture, it just wasn't going to cut it—nope, not even. The meeting lasted for hours and then it was almost like everyone took a team and divided up between the "moneys" and the "no moneys" and went to lunch to discuss more. Jory was sick to her stomach and felt totally drained. Who could eat at a time like this and on top of that act professionally? She wanted to scream at the top of her lungs as well as sit down and cry, until she couldn't cry anymore. She watched Mason through lunch and knew he had to be feeling pretty much the same. Where were they headed? Unknown to them, a lawsuit was waiting for them in the mail back at their home. Mason, Jory, John and DII all combined and individually were being sued for thirty million dollars, their company, their invention and to top it off—fraud was added to each lawsuit.

    Basically, the meeting didn't help much other than it looked like all attorneys wanted to bail. It appeared the investors would have to take the hit, but wouldn't help financially. Mason and Jory left with their tail between their legs and were totally deflated. Tension was mounting between the two of them. This was all unfamiliar territory to the both of them. When they got home Jory called her mom and dad. She needed something familiar. She had delayed in telling them things weren't going well. The negativity they usually provided wasn't what she needed, but she needed something and so hoped that maybe this time it would be different. She needed that desperately. Upon numerous occasions, if something bad was happening in Jory's life they seemed to thrive on her misfortune. Maybe, somehow, this could be support of some kind. When she finally told them everything, her dad suggested he would talk to a lifelong friend of his that was an attorney he felt trustworthy. So he did and he gave the number to Mason and Jory. No money, no company, nobody to trust, and now no attorney. Just a heap of trouble and not a clue where to turn. The mail had delivered an "urgent item" that needed to be signed for. Jory figured it must only be more "good" news.

    Todd Black was Jory's father's trusted attorney friend. Somehow she felt there may be an oxymoron in calling him that, but he was their only hope and choice at this point. Mason and Jory called and made an appointment to meet with him as soon as possible at his office in Wichita. When they picked up their "urgent" piece of mail neither could fathom the thought nor decipher what all the suits meant. The venue of all the lawsuits had been changed to Wichita, Kansas. This, too, would make it harder for all the sued parties since they would have to travel every time there was some legal gathering. The only thing they could do was to meet with Todd. They were both like zombies totally beside themselves. It was all beyond belief, but Jory couldn't deal with the "fraud" issue. What was that anyway? Who did she and Mason "fraud" anyway? It was all so confusing and incomprehensible.

The first meeting with Todd Black was at his expensive law office. When they entered the skyscraper they took the quiet elevator to the eighteenth floor. Upon entering the actual offices a whole new world was unveiled. Why is it that all law offices had an obnoxious amount of expensive marble everywhere? It was nice, but somehow disturbing to know who paid for it and how. Mason and Jory waited in the lobby for a few minutes. They overheard discussions of the same problems of other clients. It was like this was a "common" type of lawsuit. This wasn't a comforting thought. What happened to misery loving company? Instead, it was a reminder of the degradation of ethics. The meeting took a couple of hours to get the legal team set up and much to their surprise, a retainer was not needed. The law firm that had many, many prestigious clients took on this little deflated company and didn't make them pay a cent up front for a retainer. This provided a much-needed hope in insinuating the other side was indeed wrong—obviously! The firm of Black, Black and Harris felt certain they could win and would gain their fees in the settlement. That was the most encouragement either had heard in what seemed like an eternity. Their new attorneys were planning on a settlement. The one troubling point was that Mason, as well as Jory, begged to go after Matt immediately. Todd assured both of them that in due time they would depose Matt. First, certain facts and documents would have to be gained before anything like that could be done. Another disturbing point was to keep costs down, Todd would step in on the case, but it would be assigned to a young, new attorney, Jay Alton. When Jay was introduced to Mason and Jory they felt bewildered again as Jay looked all of fourteen. They tried desperately to not show their despair when they met Jay for the first time. After all, young could be good. The other difference was that Todd charged two hundred dollars an hour and Jay only charged one hundred and fifty. What a savings. Todd also spent time in explaining to Mason and Jory that people are sued for fraud to keep them from bankrupting out of the suit. If fraud is a suit then it is not possible to bankrupt without garnishing wages until the debt is paid. In this case, thirty million dollars, each, would take several lifetimes. He inquired if DII or the Gray's had insurance for this type of thing. Jory was sure they had taken out umbrella policies when the company was first formed "just in case" this sort of thing ever happened. She knew it would never be enough, but anything would help. Since they had played by all the corporate rules from the beginning taking lawyers and accountant's advice they did take out insurance for these types of problems. Todd told them to immediately call the insurance companies and get the ball rolling on that end.

    Numerous meetings took place and documents were being prepared to get to the bottom of this problem. Legal papers were drawn up to counter sue Matt Coggins, Derrik Peters, Oscar Tyler, and Jack Wilson for the exact same things. That was the rule to the game. Of course, it inflamed the whole situation right into counter suit after counter suit, dollar after dollar, anguish after anguish and nightmare after nightmare.

    Jory immediately called all insurance companies including their private insurance company that carried their personal insurance. Again, because of the "fraud" issue, they wouldn't cover them. Would the paid premiums over the last several years be reimbursed since they didn't cover the intended purpose? Of course not. Everyone from every direction was screwing Mason and Jory. It had become apparent that trusting someone, especially companies was obviously not the thing to do. From what Jory could tell by the other conversations taking place at the law firm, was that there are always other people in the same situation. What a sick society.

Todd had told Mason and Jory they could sue Rick Houser for malpractice. As sick of it as she was, in being the type of person that played by the rules, neither her nor Mason had it in them to fight another lawsuit. Even though it should have been done it wasn't in their nature to start suing everyone. Fifteen thousand dollars was looking pretty measly compared to thirty million. Todd also explained to Mason and Jory to prepare for bankruptcy mentally and to give away certain items, legally.

Of course, Todd was planning to get rid of the "fraud" issue and then Mason and Jory could go bankrupt, which would allow them to not have to pay the thirty million each. Jory felt her face turn white and the heat of her body rise. She realized that Todd thought it was good news to them that he could get rid of "fraud" and bankrupt them out of this mess. She started to sweat profusely. She excused herself while she made it to the women's restroom to throw up. Todd tried to explain that they were up against people who had an obnoxious amount of money and who ambushed the innocent for a living. Coggins and Peters looked for opportunities in crime. The umbrella, "Wilson and Tyler" were worth more than what was ever revealed. Wilson and Tyler played this game knowing the other side would never be able to stay in the game based on money alone. It looked as if Mason and Jory could be losing everything anyway, so they would play the game until the bitter end.

Business came to a screeching halt. Mason and Jory were not allowed to work in their normal capacity with either RxBot, LLC or DII. Customers continued to call and wanted more information. The attorneys had told Mason and Jory what to say and how to say it, but basically no business could take place. The bills could not be paid. Mason and Jory would no longer be paid. The Gray's world was spinning out of control. Anger levels rose at an all time high. Jory went back to the university pharmacy to work full-time. Her salary would cover her and Mason's life on a regular basis, but wouldn't cover the expense of a lawsuit. What job could ever cover the expense of a lawsuit? It worried her to be working as a pharmacist and having this kind of load on her mind at all times. Mason continued to go to DII every day because even though business didn't take place he still worked on his own to try to improve RxBot so if there was a chance he got his invention back he would be ready to go. It also kept him busy, hopeful and his mind preoccupied. This was who he was and he loved his engineering. Working on his machine was therapeutic as well as useful in the event he would be allowed to continue his dream. The lawsuit took much of the Gray's time. It practically took one of them full-time to handle all of the attorney's needs for the lawsuits—calls, faxes, e-mails, gathering documents answering questions, anything they needed. How long he could go on in that capacity was uncertain, as everything for him was.

Months were following one after another with every agonizing day. Every day was consumed with legal matters. It took several weeks for the attorneys to gather the facts and set up the case. It was costing a great deal of money. If the Gray's, DII and John Crowe didn't win then attorney fees alone would take a lifetime to pay. As the months passed, Mason and Jory begged constantly to depose Coggins. It just didn't happen fast enough. This bothered Jory on all levels. She wondered if the attorneys didn't believe her and Mason and what exactly kept them from deposing Matt immediately.

BETRAYED AGAIN

It was an extremely cold day in November. The sun was out, but it was still uncomfortable. Jory wasn't sure if it was the weather or the situation. They traveled to Wichita multiple times every week. It was time to go through some of the documents Black, Black and Harris had acquired from Coggins. It would certainly prove to be an interesting day as well as another stressful day. Hours were taken up looking through forged documents. Coggins had taken original documents and put Mason's signature on them. This was difficult to prove, but it was obvious to Mason, Jory and Jay. The trust level had dropped to an all time low for the Gray's, but they were still taken back on one of the documents more than others. Jory was going through what the attorneys had gathered and there was a letter from Scott Thomas. He was in on all of it, too?

"Oh, God, not Scott, too!" Jory exclaimed. Her heart fell and dismay took over once again.

The whole time she worked with Scott he, too, was setting them up for the stealing of the companies and RxBot.

"How could I have been so stupid," she said.

SOCKS AND PARKING PLACES

She had started struggling with this issue over and over. She could not fathom being this naive or trusting and this stupid. She absolutely hated this. Scott wrote a letter stating all kinds of untruths about Mason and Jory's activities. There wasn't anything true in it and in fact, none of the issues had ever been discussed with Scott by Mason or Jory. He was strictly hired for marketing and didn't really have any concern over the issues of the actual building of the machine or of the company. What did he have to gain from all of this? Obviously, quite a bit. The day was grueling. The ride back to Manhattan was long and quiet. Both Mason and Jory were withdrawing and trying whatever they could to get through this and to try to make some sense out of it. There was none.

DISCOVERY DAY #1

DII's discovery day took place at Todd's law firm and the attorneys had asked for all the documents from Coggin's premises before Mason and Jory were to go through them. It would take a day or two to do. It was their opportunity to see anything and everything they wanted or needed to see. Again, there were surprises after surprises of forged documents, horse farm invoices connected to RxBot business, payments to all of Coggins' family including his three daughters. Documents showing Susan Coggins approving big expenditures. Documents showing names of Coggins' secretaries approving purchases. There were issues surfacing that became obvious Matt wasn't even concerned enough to try and hide. He after all, in his devious little mind, was untouchable. He obviously was the cocky son-of-a-bitch Mason and Jory had come to know. There were papers and papers and papers to go through. They actually confirmed many of the facts of what the Gray's had told the attorneys. There were many inconsistencies in the paperwork that Coggins had given for his accounting services that it too raised a red flag for the attorneys. He would be asked about all of it when he was deposed, whenever that might be. Today would have to help speed up that process.

DISCOVERY DAY #2

D-Day #2, arrived. And it wasn't the bombing of Pearl Harbor, but discovery day for the other side. The lawsuit rules were that whatever one side did then it was the turn of the other side. It was time for Matt and Derrik's attorneys to perform discovery day at Dispensing Innovations, Inc. Attorneys would soon be plastered around DII premises going through anything and everything they could possibly get their filthy hands on. It was "their right." Their legal right—or something.

The alarm awoke Jory at six a.m. Laying there in a daze she tried not to start the day. She became more awake and into the reality of what awaited the two of them. She got up and found her furry friend at the side of the bed ready for their usual morning walk. He knew she would take him. She always did. After the refreshing damp walk, she grudgingly got ready for the dreaded day. She wouldn't be going to the pharmacy today. She and Mason were required to be at DII with their attorneys as well as making anything available for the other side. After the two were ready they decided to make a quick trip to Espresso Royale to lighten the load of the day. Espresso Royale anymore was like extended family with the routine gangs there in the morning. It always reminded Jory of the scenes from the sitcom, *Cheers*, of the crowd chanting, "Norm," upon entering the bar, but instead of "Norm" it was "Mase" or "Jory." It had become that frequently visited by the two of them.

For a few brief moments Mason and Jory enjoyed their coffee and the quiet time between them. Tensions had been mounting and to have any quiet time was much welcomed to either one of them. When they finally pulled up to DII, Jay was pulling into the drive at the same time. The Gray's and Jay got everything set up and all were trying to calm down as much as possible in the anticipation of the day. They weren't the least concerned that anything bad or unexpected would surface in the discovery because there simply wasn't anything bad to find, but all things considered it was just unsettling to have every document searched. Even the idea of the other side planting something would not be beneath them, Matt, Derrik and assumably their attorneys.

They were all upstairs when they heard the enemies arrive. Much to everyone's surprise they recognized the brutal voice that came in. It was Matts. The arrangement was to have attorneys do the discovery, but of course Matt didn't believe in attorneys or that they could do anything better than he could so he chose to do the discovery with his own staff. It was Matt, Derrik and two cheap bimbo looking assistants. They all came in three separate new white SUVs—all brand new, all identical. One of the women was the secretary of Coggins' firm. A colossal woman, with an awkward look, who hid behind a facade of paints and cheap materials. Lips naturally could not get this red or eyelids this blue without a dip into a multicolor paint bucket. This alleged woman ran interference for the CPA's. This woman had the strangest appearance. Her face was a shape not defined by definitions, but an unusual invented shape. Awkward was all one could say—nothing symmetrical. It was obvious a product of mismatched genes, and not an accident that caused this configuration. She held up one stubby hand that held two large multi-diamond horseshoe rings on her ring and pinkie finger as if directing and being head of her entourage. All of Coggins' women wore diamond horseshoe rings, a trademark of sorts. With this woman, one had to assume it was two different fingers and not just one with two rings. It was hard to see any definition in this huge woman. She was a blur, a continuous body without any delineation, a blob with diamond rings that were equally attractive. She was the type that definitely got your attention, but certainly wouldn't desire. She came with her own strong smell. A potent aroma of strong, "old lady perfume" sloshed on by the bottle. It was so strong that the stench increased exponentially when she was nearby. Immediately, Jory felt her blood vessels totally constrict. This added to the already pounding headache that could never have been imagined and it wasn't even eight-thirty a.m. The other woman wasn't anything to write home about either, but her major downfall was obviously lacking the ability to think for herself. She too had a diamond horseshoe ring on her pinky finger. What a sight of professionalism and legitimacy we had in front of us. What a freaking joke this whole scene and ordeal was.

"Can we use your copy machine or do we need our own?" were the first words that came out of Matt's belligerent mouth.

Mason, Jory and Jay all had their mouths agape and could barely believe what they were hearing, although by now should have known that he had the balls to come without an attorney.

"No, you cannot use our copier!" were the first words out of Mason's mouth.

"We have one with us, just thought I'd check," Matt"s arrogant reply echoed.

Matt's entourage followed him up the stairs and after reaching the top of the stairway Jay asked Matt, "Where's your attorney, Matt?"

Matt replied, "We aren't using an attorney."

Jay gave Matt a lengthy legal mumble jumble blurb and as Matt stood there Mason noticed how Matt's jacket bulged in the back creating a suspicious form. After looking close enough it looked like he had a holster strapped on. Mason's mind raced, but he figured Matt would have to come strapped with a gun in case an event resorted to force and it would be his one last time to prove who was actually in control of Mason and Jory's life. Why Mason didn't do something about this potentially fatal detail would someday haunt him. Today he let it go, unbeknownst on the issue of why.

When Jay finished his legal statements Matt had to once again regain the upper hand on the day so he asked Jay, "How long have you been an attorney, Jay?" The robotic entourage Matt had rounded up for the day thoroughly enjoyed the question and Jay's boy-like mannerisms as he answered the condescending inquiry. Jay really did look young even for his young age. Jory's heart fell. This justice stuff just really sucked. Their future was looking really, really grim. She didn't have the strength to care about a future, anyway not what appeared to be their future at this point. If there was a light at the end of the tunnel right now it was a freight train and Mason and Jory were right in its path.

It was a sticky humid gray Indian summer morning. For November it was odd weather. As an indicator of the day even the temperature in the building was skewed—heat everywhere. The air conditioner fan couldn't keep up. The company didn't have any extra money for utilities or limping appliances and at best the air would blow, but today being an uncomfortable day all around may have been intensified by the lame fan contributing to the stickiness of the hot thick ambient air. The morning drug at a pace of an aching stagecoach, with watching every single move the Wichita gang took. Minutes ticked away as if the second hand stuttered, finally allowing lunch to come and go without any mention of it.

It was coming upon two p.m. when Derrik said, "I've got to get some lunch," as he approached Jory directly head on and in her face. Jory subconsciously moved backwards as Derrik got closer. "Do you want us to get you some sandwiches?" he asked her.

Puzzled, flustered and engorged with rage, she said, somewhat quietly, "NO!"

Condescendingly, Derrik replied, "Don't be a martyr, Jory."

Jory literally bit her tongue and yelled at the top of her lungs, SILENTLY in her confused state of mind, "Fuck you—you bastard!"

as she didn't reply one spoken word. If she could have she would have hurt him so badly and wanted to beyond belief. She held every body muscle back as she didn't reply one spoken word. She felt the heat from her beet red face and glared into Derrik's cold satanic eyes. He eventually just turned away obviously hearing Jory's unspoken phrase as his face turned beet red. The three musketeers and their master then continued about their alleged business as if they knew what they were doing. Jory couldn't remember a headache or a stiff neck ever like the one she was experiencing at that moment. Mason wasn't doing so well either. It was becoming survival of the fittest. To each their own because it took such incredible energy to keep going and maintaining self-control that there wasn't anything left to help each other or anyone else.

When the day had finally consumed every ounce of time it could it did finally end and of course the despicable Coggins and company had copied everything possible and found absolutely nothing for their case. The organization of DII was now in shambles. It would never be the same. Jory's pain staking months of organization was now in a state of disarray. Paper was everywhere, but where it should be. Jory was literally sick, again. The day had cost DII thousands of dollars. That was one of the most expensive headaches and stressful days Jory had ever had to purchase. Unaware and speechless Jory left by herself after the end of the day. She couldn't even think. She left alone and felt alone. Mason and Jay stayed behind at DII to discuss business and to try to make some sense out of the debris left behind by Coggins.

Jory found herself back at Espresso Royale. She found it interesting that coffee was her vice and somewhat thankful she hadn't turned to alcohol or yet even a stronger drug. One of her comrades would naturally be there and she figured that was why she always returned to the place. Sure enough a friend was there. Cathy from the pharmacy was there and she pulled up a chair. Cathy could see in Jory's face that the day hadn't gone well. Cathy knew what was going on and asked about the day. Before Jory knew it she had totally spilled her guts about the day and felt a burden lifted. Venting was good and needed.

That night was tense between Mason and Jory. The tension continued to mount and was becoming unbearable. Jory found herself lying on the bed and subconsciously had not taken her sunglasses off from the day. She didn't want to be able to see anything or anyone anymore. She lay on the bed motionless and lifeless. Hobbes cuddled next to her not leaving room for any known measurement. Sleep was unheard of anymore. She always kept the Bible near. From past experiences she had noticed that when she would pick it up it would open to something that would get her to the next unbearable situation. Coincidence? She doubted it. She read and reread the Psalm phrase, "You are my hiding place from every storm in life." God was her only answer and he kept her going, even though she gave him little of her time. The time she did give, he would squeeze in a much needed answer.

DEPOSITIONS

Depositions started, but not with the main people. The attorneys started with bankers, SBA individuals, past individuals that had anything to do with the development of the machine or the forming of the companies. Again this tormented Mason and Jory. Why not depose Coggins first? Save everyone a ton of money and time AND move on. It just wasn't how the attorneys wanted to do it. Jory often thought it must be difficult for an attorney, especially if they knew they would get their money, to want to settle a case. There could be a great amount of money made from a lawsuit that wasn't settled, so why not draw it out? Hard to believe these were the people that were on their side. Mason and Jory's lives were literally in their hands. Once the depositions started, they occurred at least one a week, sometimes two. One of the problems with the depositions was that Coggins, Peters and their attorneys attended them all. They did actually have to use an attorney for the depositions. After about a half a dozen depositions, all of the stories were the same and in favor of the team they represented. It was becoming apparent that the attorney for Coggins and Peters was starting to be swayed of what was the "real" story. Even to the enemies (the Gray's) it was noticeable that Matt and Derrik's attorney believed the Gray's. This added some comfort level, but so much was needed that it barely made a dent.

It was a rainy, cold Saturday in December. Christmas was nearing which should have been somewhat distracting. Jory loved the Christmas season, but it just wasn't working for her this year. She and Mason couldn't get away from the lawsuit. Even weekends involved many phone calls to and from, Jay. Jory was fed up with everything. It had been six months of a legal battle and she couldn't take it anymore. She was never a patient person anyway, but the legal system wasn't moving fast enough. The amount of paper generated by the legal profession was almost criminal—especially from a trees perspective. What did they do with all that paper? Come to find out they had warehouses full of documents. *No shit!* Jory thought. It would take a warehouse.

She called Jay to beg for some kind of results. She was beside herself. "Hello, Jay, its Jory. Jay you gotta get me out of this, I don't care how, just get me out," she begged.

Jay tried to explain, "Jory, I can't just stop it, you are being sued personally and it just doesn't go away. I am doing everything I can to get to the bottom of this." At that point in the conversation, she had nothing more to say. Mason walked into the room and when he was within her reach she handed him the phone. She had never remembered feeling this bad. What does one do when they feel this bad and this alone? She had to scream, she had to cry, she had to get sick, she had to deal with it. When Mason got off the phone, she attacked him, physically. She had lost it.

He tried to grab her and she wasn't making any sense. She was uncontrollable. She was screaming and waving her arms to try to break loose from him. "Leave me alone, everyone leave me alone," she continued to scream between the sobbing.

That was all she truly wanted, to be left alone. If she ever got out of this mess she would never get close to anyone again—Ever. She and Mason needed to blame someone. They blamed themselves until they were mentally mutilated, but they needed to blame someone else. Sometimes, not meaning to, they blamed each other. The thought was occurring at some level for both of them, that maybe they didn't need each other if it would help get them out of this mess. Jory was losing perspective and assumed the same must be happening to Mason. On top of all the bad feelings she felt shame for the way she was handling the situation, but it just happened. The situation had gone from very bad to even worse. There was no seeing out. They were trapped in a dark battle of betrayal, which may be one of the worst kinds of battle to fight.

Christmas came and went. It wasn't the normal Christmas at the Gray's. The motions took place, but the holiday truly came and went without much attention.

During the Christmas break Mason was offered an opportunity to teach as a professor at Kansas Technical College in Salina, Kansas. Salina was an hour from his home. He went ahead and took them up on the opportunity. He could only give three days a week with the understanding he would have to be gone on certain days for depositions. The college was understanding and flexible. It offered Mason a diversion.

There was a deposition scheduled for two days after Christmas. After all, lawsuits don't take a break because of a holiday. The symbolism of Christmas didn't usually matter to people that were out to steal or destroy others. Mason wasn't able to make it to the scheduled deposition due to his teaching job. The deposition was of a board member of DII that was also a friend. When Ben Edwards was asked to be on the board, Mason and Jory thought it would be beneficial because of his father Bill Edwards, the attorney that had looked out for them for what seemed like so many years ago. Ben was a good guy, but did lack business abilities and insight. He ended up not offering much to the company. Nonetheless, he took the position without any compensation so one couldn't expect much. He was very young, too. Anyway, for some reason Coggins picked up on all of that and his side deposed him. The morning of the deposition it was overcast and freezing. The building used in Manhattan, Kansas, for this deposition was depressing. Jory arrived first and was taken into a musty, dark room. She thought that it was a fitting environment for the occasion. She found herself staring out the fifth floor window watching the pigeons. She had faded away for a few minutes when she heard someone else arrive. It was Jim Sandall, the opposing attorney. The enemy. The cold, musty room became colder and mustier. "Good Morning," he mumbled to Jory. Jory thought she responded, but wasn't a hundred percent sure. The minutes were long and agonizing as she couldn't wait for someone else to arrive on her side. Where was Jay? She actually was early so she should have expected this. Thinking ahead was out of the question anymore. Get through the moment at hand, which was all that could be expected. Somewhere from the silence there had been a conversation struck up between Jory and Mr. Sandall that turned out to be actually pleasant. Jim had somehow gotten on the subject that he attended Duke University and played football for them. How did they get to that point? It didn't really matter other than it was nice for Jory to see he was a person, or for all she knew maybe it was part of the game. The conversation didn't last long as Jay and Ben both arrived.

The deposition went horribly. Ben couldn't understand the questions to answer intelligently in any matter. It was sad because he thought he had done a good job and helped the case. Jory found herself embarrassed over the situation. It made the company look as small as they were and as inexperienced as they really were. After the deposition they went next door to Cuppa Joe's, a smoky little coffee shop. It wasn't anything like her and Mason's favorite Espresso Royale. Ben left and Jay explained to Jory what she already knew. He voiced his concern about the deposition and she knew it had a high suck level and that it didn't help them at all. They would have to try to gain some footing with the next deposition that was to be held at the offices of Black, Black and Harris in a couple of days.

When they arrived for the deposition of Nathan Roule the enemies arrived in their new vehicles. They looked like the mafia and Jory assumed that was the look they were going for. In contrast to the deflated Mason and Jory, Coggins and Peters were as cocky as ever. The deposition went very well, though. Jim, Matt and Derrik's attorney, was the one that was supposed to be doing all the talking, but Coggins couldn't keep his mouth shut. He didn't like what he was hearing. At one point, Jim lost his temper and asked for a break to have a chat with Coggins. It was amusing to the DII group. This day, too, did end after several hours and all energy expended. It had been a victory for DII, Mason, Jory and John Crowe. It was a victory, but what did that mean? Would it end the lawsuit? Coggins had to be deposed. They had to get Todd and Jay to depose him. Each side had submitted a list of who would be deposed and Coggins was near the bottom right after Peters. There were still several other people on the deposition list. If they all were deposed before a settlement and there were two scheduled a week, it would run until the end of April before Coggins got deposed. Maybe the attorneys would turn out to be competent enough to find a way to end it before the end of April.

Mason, Jory and Jay sat in the Trooper after the deposition to rehash the game plan. As they were sitting there, Coggins and his followers were leaving and acting as smug as ever. Jory couldn't take it anymore. This was getting the best of her. She was pretty sure she didn't have a best anymore. Once she and Mason were free to go, the trip home started out with idle chat. The conversation became increasingly louder as the miles passed.

"Mason, I can't do this anymore. I mean, I really can't. I have to find some way out and I am not sure anything is important enough if it can lend a way to stop this madness."

Mason pretty much just didn't respond anymore. Jory didn't know and felt like she didn't really care if he did. She was dead serious in ending this nightmare. When they arrived home it was dark and about nine p.m. Jory looked forward to seeing Hobbes. He was a bright spot. She still planned on taking him for his walk.

She yelled, "Hobbes, Hobbes, I'm home. Hobbes, come on, let's go for a walk."

There wasn't any sign of him. She was starting to get worried, but he often lay in the bushes and had gotten lazy enough to not totally respond. Usually the "walk" word worked, but maybe he didn't hear her. Mason started chiming in and it was becoming apparent that

Hobbes wasn't there. They started looking everywhere and he was nowhere to be found. Jory couldn't believe it. This couldn't be happening. Not her best friend. He had to be around, he just couldn't leave her. Mason and Jory went neighbor to neighbor and walked the park and walked the neighborhood multiple times. He was gone. One neighbor said they saw him at nine o'clock that morning, heading toward the park twelve hours earlier. Jory wanted to attack him and ask why he didn't do something since no one was with him, but she kept her composure until he left. Mason and Jory searched until midnight without any success. They called the police, but nothing could be done until the next morning to check at the dog pound. Jory wanted to die. She couldn't lose him. The thought occurred to both of them that maybe Coggins was even behind this. God knew he would stoop to any level. Jory cried and realized there were few tears left when she finally went to bed. She and Mason didn't talk much the rest of the evening. She wanted to go to sleep to allow the night to go by quickly and allow her to find her furry little friend. Where was he? Did a car hit him, did someone take him, was he lost, was he okay? It made her crazy thinking about all of it that she did finally fall asleep as exhaustion took over. The sun was coming up at around six o'clock the next morning. The pound didn't open until nine o'clock. How was she going to make it for three hours? She didn't have to be to the pharmacy until ten a.m. and she didn't care anyway. Whatever it took she was determined to find her friend.

Finally, the pound opened and when they arrived and inquired about Hobbes the nice lady said she did get a dog matching that description and to follow her. Jory wanted to hug her. Mason and Jory followed and when the doors opened, there he was. He was shivering and crying from fear. They both went over and consoled him and showered love all over him. Hobbes didn't understand when they had to leave him for a minute to go do some paperwork. The three finally had a welcomed homecoming for Hobbes. Jory was more thankful for this moment than anyone would ever know. To lose Hobbes at any time would be dreadful, but to lose him now would be inconceivable. She petted him and hugged him for the hour they had left before she had to go to work. Mason took him to Salina with him to help teach the kids. If there was a lab Mason was teaching, there were back doors to the lab and he would sometimes take Hobbes. Hobbes was extremely happy to go with Mason this time.

SOCKS AND PARKING PLACES

Knowing the odds of anything else going wrong were next to none, even though Mason knew better than to rely on that theory. Mason knew for Jory to hit rock bottom, Jory would have to jump a long ways. There wasn't a single minute, of any day, anymore, that wasn't a struggle for both of them. The deepest, darkest hole wouldn't have been any harder to get through than these days. A single step took incredible effort. To appear normal was next to impossible. To help improve the situation, Mason decided he would buy a gift for Jory. Mason bought Jory a light blue, stained glass, guardian angel, nightlight. The scene, hand painted, was the classic guardian angel overlooking a small innocent child while crossing a bridge. Jory always believed in guardian angels. Since Mason had known Jory, for as long as he could remember, she always mentioned her guardian angel and she always referred to the scene that was on this light. Deep down she believed Hobbes was somehow intertwined in that guardian angel circle. At any rate, Mason knew there could be no harm in giving her this gift. After all, a bright little light may be all it would take right now to give her a symbol of hope of something positive.

SOCKS AND PARKING PLACES

Mason had returned home after a very long day and ahead of Jory. As usual, there were several phone messages from the attorneys, multiple page faxes and numerous pieces of mail and e-mails. All had "impending doom" printed on them in some manner. Mason heard the door creak as Jory entered from her long, drawn out day. As she entered, Mason noticed there wasn't a hint of a spring in her step. She wore darkened circles under her eyes and she was looking thinner. She had a gray tinge about her these days. She took what energy she had and hugged Mason and gave Hobbes several pats and a warm hug. Hobbes had learned to hug. He would push against a leg and wag that tail, endlessly. He curled his body in such a manner that it couldn't be mistaken for anything else, but a hug. Today, his hug was a little longer than usual. The loyalty of this animal was not something anyone would believe unless they saw it with their own two eyes. Hobbes knew the true meaning of "unconditional love."

Mason took Jory by her cold hand and sat her down to give her the small, beautifully wrapped gift. Jory sighed and opened it slowly. Subconsciously, the beauty of the unopened gift, made her open it slowly to grasp any beauty she could. As she opened it, there was a big sigh from both that neither of them noticed. The tiny light, that symbol of hope, was broken. It appeared that one of the side joints had come apart. She went ahead and plugged it in only to find the light didn't work either. Tears filled her eyes and she just put her heavy head on Mason's warm shoulder.

Mason searched for strength, even though he wanted to break from the heaviness in the pit of his stomach. He consoled Jory, "Oh, baby, it's okay. Everything will be all right. We will take it back and exchange it for a new one."

The rest of the evening was quiet. It was as if no one lived in their home. It was more like a business, from which phones and faxes never stopped.

The following weekend the two of them took a couple of hours to return the broken gift. They drove several miles before entering the little stone cottage that had been converted to a gift house. Upon entering, the aroma of coffee, scented candles and wonderful cinnamon potpourri scents gave the impression that one was welcome. Jory loved these quaint little shops. She glanced at Mason with a faint smile. She always had a certain respect for owners of these businesses. They took a chance and made careers out of supplying other people with items that brought them joy. To beautify the world, even if it was commercial, was still needed. Jory's eyes brightened as she browsed around and listened to what Mason was telling the white-haired, plump, older, lady that stood behind the counter. Mason was explaining the whole situation in a calm, caring way. Jory noticed the woman didn't say anything, but, instead, picked up the phone and called someone. This seemed odd, but Jory didn't give it much thought and continued to browse around. She was finding all kinds of potential beauties. After a few minutes had passed, Jory was admiring a small candle with a small, young, precious child on the stained glass front that she had seriously considered purchasing when she was interrupted by what the clerk was saying to Mason. "This is not broken! No, it works just fine," she boastfully explained.

Mason politely listened and responded, "It is broken!" pointing to the joint. "The light doesn't work, either!" The woman walked away and returned to the phone. Mason and Jory's eyes met with a couple of questioning smiles.

The plump little woman slammed down the phone, approached Mason and loudly demanded, "You need to go next door to the liquor store and speak with Mr. Kocher, the owner." With hesitation, and surprised at the situation, Mason decided to do as she requested and to deal with the situation. The rugged neon lit shack was a few steps south of the gift shop. The liquor store was as dark, and cold as the gift store was bright and warm. *What a strange combination*, Mason thought. Mason remembered a scene from the *X-Files* that reminded him of this moment.

Mason entered the liquor store only to hear a gruff voice from the back room, "I'll be with ya inna minute."

Mason, starting to lose patience, fidgetted around until a fat, foul smelling man, with some kind of dark grotesque growth attached to his nose, appeared. Mason's first reaction was to gasp and jump back, but he kept his composure and let the man approach him, remembering that *X-Files* scene and hoping green gunk didn't start leaking out of him.

"Mr. Kocher?" Mason asked, hoping that maybe this man was the wrong person.

"Ya, whatya want?"

Mason repeated the whole incident with the light and asked Mr. Kocher to exchange the gift.

"There is nothing wrong with this light," the old man grunted.

"Mr. Kocher, look at it, not only is it broken on one side, but the light doesn't work either!" he said as he tried to demonstrate it.

After five minutes of arguing, Mr. Kocher repeated, "It's not broken. I inspected each one myself, but I'll let ya exchange it this one time."

Nothing else was said as the two of them returned to the gift shop. Mr. Kocher first, stomping through the door, Mason following with a puzzled look on his face, glancing at Jory with a smirk on his face. Jory was happily browsing, subconsciously purchasing just about everything in the shop. In her mind, she had found a perfect gift for just about everyone she knew. She saw and heard the stomping and approached the counter where the two men were standing.

Without warning, Mr. Kocher opened his mouth, "I'll exchange it this time, but I will ask you to never return."

After Jory's chin hit the floor, her eyes began to fill with tears. She gazed over at Mason to make sure she wasn't hearing things, only to see Mason's jaw also scraping the floor. Mason and Jory were totally astonished and now Mase was pissed.

After a few seconds to let the echoing of these words evaporate, Mason blurted out, "Fine," echoing with a definite attitude.

Mr. Kocher slammed down the broken light, noticing the attitude, and started shouting, "If you're going to have that kind of an attitude, then maybe I just won't exchange it."

Jory's heart was pounding, thoughts scrambling through her mind. She was totally confused. She thought to herself, *My God, this is a twenty dollar item and I just want one that isn't broken! For God's sake, it's a guardian angel—who would lie about a guardian angel?* She was beginning to believe that this is the way of this sick world. This was it! This was really how our society had become. *No!* she told herself, *it's still the Christmas season, and I'll be nice. That will work.* Jory softly responded, "Sir, this is a very nice place you have and I have found several other purchases I would like to make."

POW! A kick while she's down, a shout, "I'd rather you wouldn't! I don't need your kind. I don't want either of you to ever return to this store."

Jory, too, by this time was extremely pissed off, trying to keep her composure and to not let this monster see her cry.

"Oh, but I think you do need my KIND!" she replied. Jory had a knack for buying and spending plenty at these gift shops, obviously unknown to this moron.

Mr. Kocher proceeded to slam a new replaced light that no doubt would have to be broken also after a pounding like the one he was giving it, in the returned box and asked the two injured shoppers to leave. Mason and Jory appeared like two small children who just got punished, shuffled slowly to the door with their newly smashed night light. Neither one of them had a clue of what had just happened.

Realizing the absurdity of the whole event, Mason said with a serious face, "I've been kicked out of bars before, but never a gift store!" Laughter broke out all over the porch of the shop. They laughed so hard tears were flowing from both of their eyes. In between the hardy laughter they would repeat phrases Mr. Kocher used.

"Just what does he mean, 'My Kind?'" Jory was barely able to get the words out in between chuckles.

"This definitely hasn't been a good year," Mason retorted as he laughed. "Besides, being sued for thirty million dollars now we have become 'return fugitives.' What next?"

The laughter softened as they approached the Trooper. Mason grabbed Jory's hand as they drove away. They both analyzed the irony of that experience and wondered how are good people suppose to survive with so many malignant people loose and corrupting our society? Our society, mutating each day, evil one-step ahead of good, nothing able to eliminate or prevent its growth.

Jory's thought led to, *If only there were a cure for this sick society*. The Kocher House was about an hour from Manhattan. Mason and Jory drove the longer return drive back which demonstrated that a road could actually stretch, making the drive longer than it was earlier that day. It also became very obvious that the night was darker than most.

After a restless night, the sky was unveiling to the most spectacular purple and pinks that any morning had ever unveiled. It was worth waking up to see. Jory opened her eyes and noticed the room having a pink tint as the morning sun was peaking in the bedroom window. The morning amnesia still had Jory under its spell, making her mind empty for these first few seconds of every day. Jory had become grateful for those first few seconds of every day. She wondered if there were some way to make that amnesia period of every morning last longer. She knew this amnesia period was nature's way to keep one from waking up screaming.

As she lay there, thoughts began to return, one by one, each one more painful and darker than the previous one. Remembering the incident from yesterday she felt her heart grow heavy. There wasn't a remnant of the laughter left that she and Mason shared over that ridiculous incident. She hadn't even the strength to sit up. This was the day she knew would have to come, if indeed this terrible lawsuit, this horrific nightmare didn't end. How would she get through it? Jory had a strong appearance to all that knew her. She had been able to conceal her bad feelings, but today was different. It was impossible. She compared it to that repetitive dream in her life where she was taking an exam in a class that she never attended, and knew nothing of the topic. Though this dream panicked her, it seemed minuscule compared to the day-to-day nightmare she was now living. She didn't know how to do this day. One step at a time, but where does the energy for even the first step, come from? This feeling was so unfamiliar to her, until last June. The pit in the stomach—the isolation. She was so sure no one would ever know. It amazed her how this whole horrible ordeal could consume her. It was like someone stealing her soul, everything about her, except her shell. Except for her outside appearance, Jory, these last few months would go somewhere within. She would find several minutes had passed, many times, and when she would surface, she wondered where she had gone and for how long she had been there. Within her, thoughts would race, microsecond-by-microsecond and all so horrible. The only thoughts, now as familiar as reruns, were; *How could they do this to us? How could our legal system allow this?* And simply, *Why?* over and over until she felt the thick vomit actually fill and swell in her throat. This grotesque thickness would throw her back to the present moment and awaken her from within.

Embarrassed, but unable to control what went through her mind she even evaluated the possibility of death. After all of what was known to her, she could not imagine death would be worse. It was an option and she didn't have many these days. When this thought would creep in her mind, she withdrew for several minutes. She hated it, fought it and evaluated it the best she could. In her mind, she went one by one through all the people that meant the most to her, which ones would be effected, which ones wouldn't or minimally. At one point, she had a previous struggle with this. In that struggle, Mason was not the one who got her through it, because he was struggling and battling through his own war. Jory somehow pulled strength by remembering that horrible night. One she was not proud of, yet it was a night she wanted to forget so badly, but had to remember because it was a lesson—the lesson of her life. Somehow it contained the answer, one she had been searching for. She knew this night was shown to her as a lesson. The lesson was to remember, and to never allow herself to go there again-ever. She would make herself think about "that" night and keep it close to her to make sure it never returned.

That night's episode, Jory's darkest; the death "issue" was consuming her and was an option she seriously considered. The dreaded night was only offering tossing and turning, eliminating sleep as an option as so many nights had offered. She got up in the middle of the night, went downstairs to write Jeff a farewell letter. Jory's brother, Jeff, had always been close to her in their adult life. As kids, she terrorized him and now wondered why he gave her the time of day, but she was glad he did. He probably understood her the most and thought the most similar of anyone else in her family. He was actually a person she loved to be with because he knew how to make her laugh until she hurt. This was something she just longed for these days.

In the background the music by Genesis was playing and Jory subconsciously was listening to the words, "the key to my survival is never in ones doubt, the question was how I could keep sane trying to find a way out. Things were never easy for me, peace of mind was hard to find, I needed a way out, a place to hide...happening all the time...fear every day of what might happen that night..." Was this just irony or a message, an ill-fated ambiance, or what? Some kind of message, some kind of answer.

"Someone help me! Someone help me!" she sobbed and cried and actually waited for some answer. *God, how could this be her and how the hell did she get here?* She knew she was headed for trouble when these thoughts started happening every day; she was extremely worried what might happen that dark, struggling night. One of the big problems with the option of death was that Jory was extremely worried that this would be mistaken for an illness. Deep inside she knew it was despair. Despair was the illness, but nevertheless being labeled "mentally ill" haunted her. It was very important to Jory for people to understand she was sane. If indeed, this was going to be the answer she so badly wanted people to understand that the evil of the world did this. *Someone* evil was responsible for destroying her life. Her life had been stripped away by horrible, decaying people that survived by destroying others. Yes, she allowed them to get to her, but just how much could any one individual endure. At what point was enough? In a sense it was like a "brain washing." Every second, of every minute, of every day was consumed with these malignant organisms called humans. They were more like a flesh eating bacteria, eating cell by cell until nothing was left, no dignity and no spirit. They inflicted themselves into every aspect of her life. Nothing could be seen, heard or felt without their foul presence. All this foul presence was making her wonder if her mother was right. Her mother constantly put her down and reminded her many times that one, she was really here just for labor purposes and secondly she wouldn't amount to anything. There was never unconditional love in her life until she met Mason. Her strength in life had always been the desire to overcome these early teachings and again here it was, her only hope. Jory was often referred to as being very smart and logical by her many friends. This was an accomplishment that made her proud. This alternate opinion is what she held on to.

In her letter to Jeff, she couldn't write fast enough or explain in detail enough. She knew he would be the most understanding and she truly loved him. Her letter went on, page after page completely soaked with tears explaining what she was feeling, her questions and ending it with how much he had meant to her and how much she loved him. It was completely unknown to her that the body could actually cry and release this much emotion. After she could no longer write, exhausted, she tried to quit sobbing, but she just placed her head in her hands and begged for someone to help. Mason was upstairs sleeping, unable to hear, unable to help. God, she needed help so badly, but didn't know who would ever understand. She always appreciated her faith in God and that God was by her side. These days she felt so alone and there were just no answers to be found. Her trust still remained in Mason, Jeff and of course, God. Although shaken, the trust was still there. Where was God now? When Jory felt herself slipping into these horrible times, many a night she would search and search in that Bible for answers. It was consistent in helping her find temporary relief. But tonight she was alone, she was sure of it. It was so cold, so dark and no sign of life, no visible signs of answers. What was all of this for? Although, she felt abandonment, ironically the only reason she never chose the death option, was her faith in God. With all the uncertainty in her life, she was worried that there may be a very good chance that the theory she had been taught all of her life, that suicide was an unforgivable sin, might just be right. That was a huge risk. The biggest one yet. Another problem with this theory, however, was that it was also taught to her that God would never give anyone more than they could endure. Where is the logic to this, people did indeed kill themselves so that disproved that theory, for Jory. She tore up the letter to Jeff in a million pieces. Exhausted, she fell asleep at her desk. No one ever knew about the darkest, hardest night of Jory's life. She was never fully aware of the intent of that letter, was it a release or one step closer to leaving her life? The connection that letter was to Jeff, that treasured trust, gave her strength. She knew Jeff would never know about this, but she would be forever grateful to him because somehow he was there with her that night and in a sense, he saved her life.

In the early morning of that horrible night she reached a turning point. She woke up, heavy, barely able to move. Subconsciously, aware that emotional distress must be the most exhausting form of a workout that exists. She stumbled around and found her way back upstairs to bed. She rolled over, tears rolling down her cheeks, sobbing quietly. She watched Mason to see if he was awake. Even while Mason slept, his once carefree beautiful face was now marred with such anguished, such tense expressions. At the first moment when he awoke, when most are rested, Mason had dark circles under his eyes. Mason was a sleepwalker, especially under stress. Many nights he would awake in total terror. Screaming, sweating and either saving someone or running from something. Once consciousness would take over, not a trace of the dream would remain. Mason never had a clue as to what had taken place in one of his nightmares. These weren't like the events that had taken place in his younger more carefree days. These dreams used to be a source of laughter and jokes. Their favorite "night terror" was when Mason was taking calculus in college. In the middle of one night, Mason was at the foot of the bed, yanking, pulling, shaking, and presenting himself as the terrorist to the poor defenseless mattress.

Abruptly awakened, heart-pounding, Jory saw the dark figure at the foot of the bed and asked, "Mason, what are you doing, for God's sake?"

"I'm looking for variables x and y," he would answer. This was only one of the many, many adventures of Mason's sleep patterns over the years.

Mason awoke, but kept his eyes closed to keep the day from starting. As with every dreaded day, lately, he prayed to keep a continuous sleep cycle going—whether it was peaceful or not. After all, if it wasn't peaceful, he would never remember. Sleep became an escape. There was a longing for those dreams that could take you far away to a wonderful serene place, where the soft colors were indescribable and the people were laughing, enjoying life and were flawless—the kind of dream that when awakened, the remnant would carry you through the day.

Wanting to release all the bad memories, Jory brought herself back to the moment at hand and back to reality once again. Barely awake, she managed to get up and stumble around to get ready for work. She assumed *that* night she had revisited was her worst and now here was that unavoidable day that would eventually have to come. It was the inevitable. Struggling with each movement, one foot in front of the other, step by step, each piece of clothing, one piece of thread at a time covering one piece of her body, each breathe stressed with long periods between each inhalation and tripping over towels that had been dropped and articles of clothing that had been strewn everywhere only to realize how much of the housework was unfinished and ignored these long, hard days. She slowly went downstairs to the cold laundry room to go through the monumental heap of clothes to find a pair of socks.

This alone looked as if it would be an insurmountable task. Much to her surprise and relief, there was a pair of socks right on top. Without noticing, Jory released a big sigh. She continued to get ready and rushed to work. She had the everyday task of trying to find an available parking spot. Finding parking at the university was as likely as swimming the widest part of the ocean. There was a joke among co-workers that employees paid eighty-five dollars per year for a hunting license. Jory always made jokes upon entering the pharmacy. "I parked at Dillon's Supermarket," she would chuckle, which meant about five miles from work. Or another favorite was "forty-five miles west."

SOCKS AND PARKING PLACES

Today was different. Heart heavy, little energy she took a chance at a close parking spot. "My God!" she mumbled. "There's a spot!" Without noticing, she let out another huge sigh.

She turned off her Trooper and analyzed the day to this point. She began to cry, uncontrollably. She suddenly realized, at this point, her life had so many negative forces in it that finding a pair of socks without looking and finding a close parking spot was all she had to hold on to today. She was thankful. After all, it didn't matter what it was as long as there was something to hold on to. She recomposed and thought of how God worked in such mysterious ways. Always trying to be what she perceived God wanted her to be, Jory was not a ritual church going person, but today and many days she paid attention to God's signs. Like a roadmap, if you paid attention then surely you would end up in the right place. Somehow she knew that she had come through the darkness, she would survive, and she would find freedom once again. Her dignity and spirit would someday return. She had to believe this. This was her hope. She laid her head back for a few seconds and thanked God for socks and parking places.

POINT OF NO RETURN

Mason was filling most of his time at Kansas Technical College, teaching engineering classes. This took his mind off of everything, briefly. Since the lawsuit limited his options professionally, restricting him from working in his area of expertise, except in the teaching capacity, he really had no other choice. He had come to enjoy the change and was thankful for at least one option. The contrast of teaching to owning and running his own company was like night and day. Jory started using the analogy as "feeling bi-polar" because it was extremely opposite of his usual working capacity. Being an entrepreneur was not flexible, not relaxing or low-keyed, in fact, not that enjoyable. Teaching was flexible, was relaxing and low-keyed. It was getting him out of the house, something he and Jory both enjoyed anymore. Mason was viewed as an exceptional teacher. He related extremely well to the young students. The "hands-on" experiences he provided would lead him to a "Teacher of the Year" award within two years and a nickname of the "Pied Piper" because when Mason Gray walked down the hall, his students would be in a line following him. He was meeting new people and developing a separate life from that malevolent place previously known as home. He was surprised about his newfound feeling of wanting to avoid home. It had always been a place he looked forward to returning each day. Not anymore.

Kayleen Lewis was a secretary in the engineering office. Mason had come to know her well over the past few months. She was a single mother, twenty-eight years old, under-educated and recently divorced. She had a nice way about her and wasn't bad to look at either. Mason and Kayleen had many conversations these days and compared their loneliness to one another. It was becoming apparent that the time they were spending together at work was leading to a possible mutual relationship. Without either one being extremely forward, there was some attraction between them. Mason and Jory were having trouble taking care of each other these days. Each was individually surviving by whatever means. They neglected each other. It wasn't intentional, but rather a form of survival. It resulted in total loneliness. Mason thoroughly enjoyed the sex he and Jory had together. They used to joke about Mason's love for sex between them. Mason would explain to Jory it was the way he was wired that continuously made him want her. Mason had an engineering spin to everything. Now, all of that had become memories. The distance between them was continually expanding. Time, stress, and emotional barriers were tearing Mason and Jory apart. The hurt of that, alone, was enough to make both of them emotionally unstable.

Mason had noticed the differences of Kayleen and Jory numerous times. Somehow this was part of the attraction. Something, someone completely separated from his present life. He realized that when men cheat on their wives it is usually with women who are completely opposite of their spouses. He could now understand why. He knew women like Jory would never allow themselves to be available or vulnerable like Kayleen. This was comforting and unnerving. Comforting for the spouse, but it took on a completely different meaning when the spouse was inviting the thought of becoming an adulterer.

Days had turned into weeks, weeks into months of small chat and much needed company between Mason and Kayleen. It was Friday and lunch time. Mason and Kayleen had been in the back copy room. Kayleen was making overheads for Mason's afternoon class. "Are you doing anything for lunch, Mason?" Kayleen asked in a requesting voice.

"I don't know," he answered with hesitation. "Why?"

Kayleen softly spoke and explained to Mason, "I only live five minutes from here. Why don't you come over and I will fix you one of my famous roast beef sandwiches."

Mason was quiet for a second and suddenly realized that Kayleen really did look attractive today. He had noticed her presence earlier in the day, but not like now. She was wearing a tight, blue, low cut t-shirt. Her cleavage was forcing her large breasts to only be covered half-way. Her skirt, short and tight, was extremely inviting.

"Yeah, okay, I'll be ready in fifteen minutes. I'll follow you over to your place, okay?" he replied. Both knew exactly what this lunch meant.

Mason's mind was racing as he followed Kayleen to her modest trailer court. Mason was questioning who he was. Had his life changed enough that he was going to give it all up. He didn't want to think anymore. He just wanted to get to Kayleen's and go inside.

Both arrived within seconds of each other, Mason following Kayleen into her trailer home. It was quiet; no word was spoken, creating a foreign, awkward atmosphere. As they entered, Mason froze at the entrance. He noticed the small spaces and the unique smell that belonged solely to a trailer home. He wanted to enter and run away all at the same time.

Kayleen entered the kitchen and noticed Mason's hesitation. He was still standing in the doorway, frozen, as she asked him, "You're not going shy on me are ya? Mason, this is not a commitment, only a solution to our loneliness. Please come in."

Mason's mind was still racing and refused reality to provide logic. *God*, he thought, how he really wanted this—and Jory. He immediately pushed Jory out of his mind and focused on the moment at hand. His body was definitely giving him the go-ahead, but his heart was interfering. Kayleen walked towards him and grabbed his hand and forced him over to a chair. She put her hands on top of his shoulders and pushed him down to sit. She kneeled in front of him, leaning forward and brushing the insides of his thighs, forcing him to be fully aware of her large breasts. She started to lift up her shirt when Mason jumped up. Kayleen jumped up, too, and grabbed him. He grabbed her and held her close. At that moment he realized this couldn't be. He couldn't cross that line. One more step and he would be at the point of no return. He was losing his entire life. Did he want Jory included in that loss?

He hesitantly and sadly responded, "No, I can't do this, I have to go. I am really sorry, Kayleen."

Kayleen, with tears in her eyes, quietly spoke, "I wish I would have been married to someone as dedicated as you."

As Mason drove away he knew he had made the right decision. His marriage wasn't based on sex alone. He and Jory had something very special, something so rare among couples these days. Granted, it was strained, but it had to still be there, it really had to still be there. He wasn't willing to throw it all away for one steamy lunch. He had always reassured Jory he would never cheat on her. He believed it when he made that promise to her, but he had never actually been in a situation to carry out the test. When it got down to the bottom line he wasn't absolutely sure what he would do. So many days lately, his morals, beliefs, his entire life were being tested. Turning to a life of women, sex, and no commitments didn't sound half bad at this point. Having no responsibilities could become very attractive. Mason knew this was a surface need and not a life long dream of his. He made the right decision and it felt good. There were so few people Mason could trust these days and Jory was one of the few. He knew he could trust her implicitly. He knew she must be going through some of the same decisions these days and for a split second he felt a sinking pain in his gut hoping she would also choose to stay with him. Mason had noticed Jory had deteriorated over the past year and he didn't want to destroy the little bit of trust she had left in him.

As he was driving and evaluating his decision, he suddenly realized the tears running down his cheek and whispered, "God, what is happening to my life?" He too, had never remembered feeling so alone and lost.

NULLIFY IN COURT

More and more months continued to pass with the legal game becoming routine and part of the Gray's daily lives. They were somewhat over the initial shock, but the day-to-day drama was still unbearable. Both had come to realize that they had no choice, but to deal with it, get it over and survive. Coggins continued to twist the agonizing knife. Mason and Jory went to the National Pharmacy Meeting in March as they normally did. Both had looked forward to the time away. Here it had already been a year since the last meeting with Seth, when all suspicions were laid out on the table. Apparently, Mason and Jory took the wrong path. When they arrived at the beautiful hotel in Nashville, Tennessee, Jory saw old classmates from the University of Texas. She actually didn't want any contact with any people except Mason. Times were stressed and she hoped for some kind of breakthrough. The trip would prove to not be a breakthrough, offer no time or relaxation, and absolutely no time without stress. She and Mason had just finished dinner when they were walking around enjoying the scenery. After dinner, they picked up a schedule for the meetings and events for the following days. Jory stopped cold in her tracks. She couldn't speak.

Mason thought something medically was wrong. "Jory, what's wrong?"

By that time they had arrived at their room and she was hysterical. "Look at this, Mason, they are here with RxBot."

Coggins, Peters, and Scott Thomas had broken all the rules again and brought the machine under the RxBot name. They were listed as the company RxBot, LLC, to be an exhibitor at the national meeting, demonstrating the machine RxBot. Jory continued to be surprised that she took these hits, feeling worse than the previous ones. Every single time she thought there was no way she could feel worse. She realized one really shouldn't say "never" or "things can't get worse!" The phrases were like curses. She broke down worse than ever. Mason became glued to the telephone, desperately trying to reach Jay or Todd to see if there would be anyway to stop Coggins, et al., from being an exhibitor for the following day. It was Friday night, which couldn't be an optimum time for catching any of the legal team.

A court order by Saturday. *Yeah, right,* he thought to himself, but he continued to try. He sat in the oversized hotel chair dialing or holding his head in his hands. He had to alternate each action until he reached Jay. He finally did reach Jay. Jay explained that Mason and Jory would have to live with it for the agonizing moment. It would become part of Coggins problem when they finally reached court and it wouldn't be good. "Nullify in court! God," Mason thought how both of them hated hearing that anymore. Jory withdrew the rest of the night and cried the entire night. She was exhausted and felt destroyed. She did however find the nerve the next day to go to the exhibitions and went straight to the RxBot exhibit. Scott's face turned white when he saw her. There were tons of people watching the machine. Their expressions were favorable. Jory was always proud to watch the machine, until now. It was however, still an awesome machine. Pharmacists were excited about it. Jory thought and thought before she acted. She wanted to kill Scott. She really did want to inflict personal harm on him, but she needed to be professional. She could maintain professionalism, but put him on the spot to gain information.

"How many of these systems have you sold? What kind of support do you have? How many are up and running now? If I wanted one, how soon could I get one? How fast does it fill a prescription? How does it work?" were a few of her questions, the latter being her favorite because she understood his *real* intelligence level. Of course, he had taken lessons from Coggins and had answers for everything she asked, but she could tell he was sweating. That alone gave her the satisfaction she so desperately needed for the moment. She backed off and left. She and Mason left Nashville even more deflated. Hard to imagine there was such a state.

Distraught as ever, Mason got up early to return to his teaching. As he backed out of the garage, he and Jory hit the garage door opener at the same time making the garage door come down on top of the Trooper. Mason yelled at the top of his lungs, "God-Damn, Son of-a-Bitch, Fuck!" Jory was sure every single neighbor in a five mile radius had heard him. He lost it and Jory was relieved to see some emotion from him. This lawsuit nonsense had taken its toll on Mason, too, but he had resigned to quietness rather than showing any emotion. Jory felt really bad for him. Both dealt with the garage door and went on their miserable ways. The garage door symbolized what they felt, twisted, unstable, and completely out of sorts.

CHECKMATE

May 1st. May day, a day for May baskets, flowers, and unexplained beauties left on the front porch followed by an unexplained ringing of door bells, and two days before Jory's birthday. Joyfulness, excitement, new hope of a new month and season. Not today. Instead of birthday plans, in two days Coggins would be deposed on May 3rd. Finally. The attorneys were able to prolong his deposition not only until the end of April, but right into May. Although, it had potential to be the best birthday present ever if the truth finally did unfold and a settlement took place. Mason and Jory couldn't be anymore anxious. They couldn't be anymore, anything! It was at that critical point—all or none. It would be Mason and Jory losing everything or gaining everything. Which would it be? The decision of their lives was being made by the powers that be. This was it. How would Coggins do it? Could he pull it off like the OJs, and the Clintons of the world? He was evil, but could he conceal it one more time, effectively? This was the one thing the Gray's begged for on the first day of this horrible nightmare and numerous times since.

Please just depose Matt Coggins first! It will tell you everything you want to know! If you doubt us then go for him, but please do it now!

One year later, one hundred fifty thousand dollars later, the attorneys would now depose him. This was it. The end was near. This was how the judicial system worked. If Coggins would have been deposed at the beginning of this ordeal then how would the attorneys have made the one hundred and fifty thousand dollars? No, the process had to be drawn out. To think these attorneys were our allies. It had become a joke to think that attorneys could be anyone's allies when, in fact, the two terms did prove to be an oxymoron. One underlying truth was that Mason and Jory got to this point because of attorneys. From the first day of this invention they *knew* they couldn't go forward without them. Now, they were totally relying on them to uphold the documents they had created.

The biggest probability was that Coggins would do anything possible to prevent being deposed. He had used every scare tactic available. Mason and Jory seriously doubted he would ever be deposed, but then what, they knew he wouldn't give in either.

The anxiety was overwhelming. Nausea, tempers, tears, withdrawing, loneliness, rage and mostly, uncertainty were all heightened this afternoon. Time was running out. If Coggins did get deposed then that was good. Everyone involved, believed the truth would come out. On the other hand, if he didn't get deposed it could also be good, lending to the idea of a settlement. Comfort was in these thoughts just knowing something had to happen today. It was checkmate?

May 2nd. Four forty-five p.m. The phone rang. Mason and Jory looked at each other, letting the phone continue to ring. Both knew what that phone call could mean. Mason hesitantly answered, "Hello."

"Mason, it's Jay. They want to settle. Eight hundred thousand dollars with them getting everything that belongs to the company. Mase, are you there?"

"Yeah," Mason quietly answered with a million thoughts racing through his mind. "Jay, why didn't we depose him or threaten to depose him earlier? I knew he would never let you question him or his abilities."

There was no answer. All of the involved parties knew the answer.
"Okay, it's a start, but we will never settle for that amount."

After hours and hours of negotiating, it was ending. The final settlement was Coggins would pay the Gray's two million dollars for their patent and technology in exchange for the company and everything the company owned. Mason did in fact make it to be a millionaire and it mattered little that he was thirty-six.

After agonizing hours on the phone and working out the details it was finally, really over. Mason and Jory discussed among each other and all investors what should be done in these final moments. It was really ending. Mason explained to the investors that they would be paid back proportional to their percentage of ownership. This wasn't a legal requirement. The attorneys indicated the Gray's could keep all of the money. Mason knew he had to give the investors their money back for their support and trust. He never even gave it a second thought.

Realizing it had gotten late, Jory needed fresh air badly. She went outside to get the mail. As she reached into the mailbox she grabbed what she thought was a magazine only to find one of her latest *Pharmacy Topics* journals dated April twenty second. Blood running from her head, heart racing, both very familiar feelings these days, she read as fast as she could. On the front cover was Mason's machine. The headlines read, "RoboR.Ph", next to a crisp picture of the brilliantly designed cell.

"Damn, he had it planned to the bitter end!" she whispered to herself. Now knowing the ending of the story, she and Mason would make a great deal of money, but Coggins would still actually win. Remembering the saying she had now become so familiar with, "in a legal battle, NO ONE wins." Slowly walking back towards the house, energy drained she sat on the front porch for a few minutes to catch her breath. She noticed among the chill in the air an amazing glow of pink and turquoise enveloping the earth beginning another spectacular sunset. The world almost had to end for her to not notice a sunset and ironically it almost did.

For a brief moment, Jory slipped away, thinking how this ordeal reminded her of a rafting incident she had in Texas. One very hot summer day a few years earlier, she, Mason and four friends had all decided to go tubing on the Gruene River in New Braunfels, Texas. Brad, a college buddy and a close friend had convinced the two of them that tubing this river would be an experience to remember. That it was. Unknown to all of the tubing buddies, the river was too high to use for entertainment. It was too high with the enormous amount of recent rainfall. The crowds didn't display concern of any sort, to this fact—ignorance is bliss. After an hour of winding roads, friendly chatter and plans for the day, all exited the car with fury, sweating from the balmy, humid morning. There were people everywhere, adding to the excitement of the new adventure. With a throng this large it could only mean it was all right to tube these high waters, after all could so many people be wrong about one thing? The excitement compared to a group of small children waiting for their first swimming lesson. The six of them, Mason, Jory, Brad, Brad's wife, Annie, and two other friends Fitz (short for Fitzmeir) and Amanda, Fitz's wife, acquired all the gear they needed, which ended up being coolers and inner tubes. After all, what more is needed to float down a river? Life jackets weren't required because, "One could walk anywhere in the river, it wasn't that deep," Brad had convincingly explained.

Jory wondered to herself, *Why is it when a friend tells one something, it is very seldom doubted, to much of any degree?* Subconsciously and against her better judgment she blew off the logic to evaluate that little noted fact.

All six gleefully entered the river at the west bridge and on the small black inner tubes they jumped. The laughter caused laughter in itself.

"Oh, my God, this is awesome," Jory roared as she took off down the river.

The river grabbed on to each individual adopting an attitude and providing a ride none would forget. All friends taking their own path, all started to separate. The water was roaring and spewing from the boulders and approaching at the speed of lightening.

SOCKS AND PARKING PLACES

Laughter, excitement, "Hold on, here comes the first big one!" yelled Brad.

Jory waved her hand at the huge boulder as she approached it, as if she were in control. Smack! It was as if she had been knocked out. The next thing she knew she was totally immersed in strange waters. She was trapped under the water and everything was murky green. She knew immediately this was part of drowning. She was caught in an underwater tornado. The current had captured her. Jory, being a competent swimmer, used her swimming ability to save her life, not by swimming, but understanding one has to respect the waters to survive. She made herself go limp, bumping back and forth into boulders and scraping against foreign objects. She felt as if she were in a washing machine on the heaviest cycle being agitated back and forth.

After what seemed like minutes, seeing and living a whole, strange, murky, world, she was thrown out to sunlight. She was gasping for air and faintly saw an elderly gentleman in a kayak. He was holding out a much appreciated hand and she could hear him, "You're okay. Hold on, I've got you, hurry, hold on!"

Coming to a much-needed consciousness, she noticed all the people being saved in the same manner by other kayaks. It took but just a couple of seconds to realize, Mason was gone. He was nowhere to be found. Panic sat in. The kayak held on to her through the rushing river and took her to calmer waters.

Extremely panicked, she looked for a familiar face, "Oh, my God, what is happening?" She looked across the river only to see the kayaks throwing ropes to stranded people that were stuck on top of boulders that only had raging rapids between the boulder and safety. "Mason, Mason, where are you?" somewhat in a whisper she called his name over and over. As she frantically called, raising her voice with each sound, she searched for Mason. As she was searching, a young woman, face down, went floating down the river.

In the background, she heard a man's voice, "Someone help her. She can't swim!" As frantic as Jory was, she was able to realize how ridiculous this entertainment was to someone who could not swim, let alone, those who could. A man did jump in and save the woman. He took her to the side of the river and performed CPR. "She's okay!" she heard someone else scream. Jory heard and saw the whole bizarre incident taking place as she slipped along the muddy shore, searching everywhere for Mason.

She spotted a face that was so comforting, but he was as white as a sheet and the faint distant words coming from his sweet pale mouth were, "Jory, Jory, where are you?"

Mason spotted Jory and then they both ran towards each other. They were both talking at the same time, trying to examine what had just happened. "You were right by me and I saw you go in so I went in after you," Mason explained. "I was thrown way out and lost you, God, I thought you had drowned. Thank God you're okay!"

Jory was shivering, terrified and cried, "Mason, I couldn't find you anywhere, I was so scared!"

They both held on to each other, strolling along the edge of the water to find their friends.

They finally met up with Fitz. One could always count on Fitz to lighten any occasion. Unaware of any danger, he had his snorkel on, collecting all the debris; tubers were losing in the ferocious rapids. "Jory, what size shirt do you wear?" he asked and under the water he would go. He surfaced with florescent, foot long sunglasses, bottles of beer, coolers, sandals—a regular little flea market under the water. Unable to escape the laughter Mason, Jory, Fitz, and Amanda got somewhat back into the spirit of things. Brad and Annie came about five minutes later. They had been two of the few who made it through the raging rapid without to much difficulty. They did, as one should, stay on their inner tube. Stories were shared, frightfulness diminishing and all rested on the shores. Fitz continued to shop for everyone.

Jory, explained, "Okay, Nielson, you owe us an explanation. What do you mean, the river is shallow, no life jackets are needed and you can walk anywhere?" Although, Jory was joking once again, she was scared to death to go on.

Brad excitedly grabbed Mason. "Come on, Mason, let's go back through that first one. She's a bad ass, isn't she?" Mason knew if he didn't go right then he, too, wouldn't want to continue. Jory couldn't believe her eyes. Mason did go with Brad and successfully made it through the second time, without incident. They stayed on the inner tube. It was becoming obvious that if you could cling tight enough to the inner tube, staying above water could be accomplished. Jory watched and shook her head, insisting on walking a ways and avoiding the rapids while the others went on. Oh, that sounded like a great plan, but Brad had failed to provide one tiny piece of information that was vital for surviving the day. Brad wasn't sure how far the river went for tubing and where one could exit. He did know it was all private property and that no one was allowed to walk the shores. And one could not turn around and go back to the beginning. Hours and hours went on, rapids were everywhere, Jory tried to walk the river has much as she could, but every time she tried, it got to wild and deep. She was shivering, not from the cold, but from the adrenaline. Her skin looked like a plucked chicken with all of the goose bumps. Every time she heard the sound of the rapids, she felt her body begin to quiver. She walked to the rapid on one of the sites and made it to a tree only to find people watching their canoes split apart by the water.

Again voices were screaming, "Help, Help!" as people would try to hold on to trees as half of the canoe would go floating away, throwing out the castaways. A raft went crashing into a raging rapid. A young woman was all that was left of the inflatable raft that previously held two other victims. The frightened woman held out her hand to Mason, who was now standing on the shore. He grabbed her raft with one hand while the other was holding on desperately to a twig of a tree. The waters were rushing horrifically. He was spread out like Wile E. Coyote after being demolished by the roadrunner. Failing to help, the eyelet of the inflatable float broke away, snapping Mason backwards on to shore and sending the isolated woman away into the haunting raging waters. The river owned this castaway. Some were lucky enough to grab something concrete on the shore while the "kayaks" saved others again. As Jory was holding on to a tree she learned from another survivor that the kayaks were civil defense and even though people were allowed to tube, the waters were at flood stages. Jory wondered how she could have been so stupid.

In Texas, multiple times, the facts were pushed to the side and appearance masked a current situation by, "Well, if this many people are doing it, it must be okay."

She quickly thought of her mother saying, "If your friends jumped off of a bridge, would you?" This whole scene was a natural disaster. Not fun, not entertaining, but a freaking disaster. People were drowning and being saved, everywhere.

Jory jumped from the squealing voice! "Get off my property, NOW!" exclaimed the angry owner.

For God's sake, she thought as she was holding on to a flimsy tree—holding on for dear life!

"You get off my property NOW!" the owner demanded, again.

Everyone tried to wade as far as they could. Jory carefully walked on the slippery, mossy-covered rocks. Mason followed her on foot. He was definitely concerned, but he was much better at seeing the adventure of this escapade than she was. Finally, the river widened, calming the waters. Jory was still shivering, calming to a quiver comparable to an earthquake measuring five on the Richter scale. This so-called calming allowed her to get back on her inner tube just in time to notice she had something slimy, cold, and dark all over her. For a moment, she thought it was mud and then she let out a squeal that life on Mars could have heard, "Oh, shit, baby snakes, all over me. Get them off!"

She jumped into the water, hysterical, and with a moment to focus she figured out what was thought to be baby snakes were actually leeches. Like that was supposed to be of some comfort. Three hours of "fun-filled" adventure had passed. She survived five or six rapids, multiple leeches, and adrenaline surges at toxic levels only to look up and see a "think" sign that showed where some poor soul drowned diving into shallow water.

Jory piped up, "Obviously, that poor sucker didn't drown in this freaking shallow water! Brad, I will never forgive you for this one!"

Brad gave her an ornery sneer, jumped off his inner tube and swam toward the shore, bumping into Jory's inner tube, spilling her into the water.

Mason yelled, "Nielson, you crazy son-of-a-bitch, what are you doing?" Ahead of them was a tree swing.

"Does the *fun* just never stop?" Jory griped.

The whole gang went to the shore. One at a time, taking turns, each one acquiring their own, unique technique, swung from the tree rope out over the water and dropped, making a huge cannonball-like splash. All were laughing and screaming before each one submerged. For about an hour, the group played in calm waters, which helped tremendously. Truly, not knowing how much more of the river one had to go they all decided they better keep heading east. Jory began to shiver again. She realized she could not shiver any more if she was placed on ice for hours. After six long, agonizing hours, the end was in sight. The end bridge. Finally! Safety! Relief! There was one big problem. To get to the bridge one had to pass through the biggest, baddest, rapid, yet. Oh, with this bridge and final rapid, there wasn't just one problem, but two bad ass problems. First, could one actually make it through the rapid and live? Second, to keep from getting decapitated, one would have to go to the extreme right or left, in a short amount of time before hitting the "low water crossing" bridge. The water was completely to the top of the bridge with some spilling over and covering the surface of the bridge. The problem with all of this was there was no navigating allowed through the rapids. The river navigated you. It controlled you. If it said drown, well, then you would drown.

"That's it! No fucking way!" Jory yelled. Jory usually didn't have this fowl of a mouth, but this was it. "I will pay any amount of money one wants to fine me, but I am not going through this rapid."

As Mason and Jory were trying to work out a plan, Mase wasn't too excited about this one either as he watched someone heading straight for the bridge. The poor, out of control, tuber put his head completely back to keep from being decapitated as he went under the submerged bridge. As he reached the bridge, he had his head totally submerged, backwards. After a few seconds, a survivor on top of the bridge went to the other side to see if the submerged tuber made it. Every spectator was breathless, quiet taking over as everyone was anticipating the result.

After what seemed like an eternity, the survivor exclaimed, "He made it!" The whole crowd cheered.

Mason could hardly believe what he was seeing. He actually chuckled, as he, too, couldn't believe the predicament they were in and that they had actually chosen it. "Jory, I don't know if we can make it walking, either, since the water is so rough."

"Watch me," she demanded.

Her mother used to remind Jory that the one thing she and all of her siblings had in common was their "strong will." To date, this was the biggest compliment that had been given to her. Normally it pissed her off, but today she would use it in the most positive way and make it work for her. She struggled, one leaded leg after the other, walking forcefully against the raging waters. Finally, meeting the shore with demanding homeowners, pointing, standing on their property protecting it from the desperate tubers, she entered their property. Mason was behind her and they both literally ran for their life to public property. Six hours and fifteen minutes later, the *fun* was over. Exhaustion had set in. A long ride home, all friends were in tact and sharing war stories of the day. Margaritas and Mexican food at Las Famile were graciously waiting their arrival. Las Famile was one of Austin's best Mexican restaurants and was famous to this group. Their friendships had always been great, but life was more precious at this moment because they were all survivors of the raging rapids of the Gruene River. Everyone wanted to put a fun twist to the day, but Mason and Jory knew what they had done and what they had come through. Drowning was enveloping them. Death was near by and had lurked over them all six very long hours. Danger was absolutely present and they made it. After the day was over and the darkness of the day sat in, darkness sat into their soul. They focused on how they could have lost everything in one raging rapid—their life and each other. Jory realized she was daydreaming about a choice she and

Mason had made in their younger, more adventurous days and had survived after what seemed like an eternity, not much different than today by losing control of their life. Although the analogy was similar, this lawsuit was evil and she knew, in a sense, they had drowned. That phone call today had sent them the kayak to save their lives.

GUARDIAN ANGEL

May 29th, Mason and Jory's seventeenth wedding anniversary. Both were wondering if they could make it to this day and if either would be able to feel anything ever again. The numbing from the lawsuit experience was as if the two of them had been submerged in sub zero temperatures for the past year and the thawing from it would take an eternity, if possible at all. Both were hoping the damage was temporary, but the two of them knew this would not be the case. Damage these criminals did would never go away, but Mason and Jory wanted more than anything to be able to move forward with minimal bitterness. They had been blown off course this past year. Whatever happened to that road map with all of God's signs popping up at every corner? Jory had believed in those signs with all of her heart and soul and for all of her life. A wrong turn is what it was or so it appeared. A turn that had changed their lives—an unwarranted trust. The way they viewed people, their attitudes, their confidence, their visions and their dreams would never be the same. It was a knowledge gain that would change their entire ways. What were they going to do with this new knowledge gain? A knowledge neither of them wanted. One could only hope it was for the better, but it obviously wasn't all positive. Damage control was what was needed now. Jory couldn't even look at people in the same way. She was never a reserved person, but, instead, a very open and accepting person. Now she wasn't either of those, but, rather, reserved and distant. She despised her new feeling of "caring so little" about people in general. Or maybe it was being apathetic rather than non-caring, either way it was foreign. She didn't like it. She had no patience for anyone, especially the manipulative. She knew the only thing that could define it was that she had been sued for thirty million dollars, for something she and Mason invented and owned—PERIOD. Their lives had teetered from the possibility of bankruptcy to possibly gaining much wealth for the last year with bankruptcy appearing as the winner, most of the time. Not just bankruptcy, but losing everything at hand. It wasn't just a matter of money. The money aspect of it all created a tremendous amount of stress, but losing everything, absolutely everything, right before their eyes, even things that had nothing to do with this ordeal, was next to impossible to fathom. It was truly unbearable. And to see whom it was going to was retching. All the legalities in the world wouldn't change the root of the truth. Mason and Jory had every right to everything they had fought for. It was theirs from the beginning. In reality, it was theirs, there was no fighting for it, and they had always owned it. How could they be forced to fight for it when they *were* the *creators* of the dispenser? This is what made it all so difficult for Jory. She always saw everything in black and white, right or wrong. This is *not* how the legal system worked. It was all gray, except the green that lined the attorneys' pockets.

Mason's attitude had deteriorated over the past year as to be expected, but something about him was definitely different. The easygoing, carefree man was gone. The soft, warm face had hardened and the experience had hardened him, but yet he wasn't cynical. Jory loved him immensely, but she was saddened to see what had happened to him. She understood what made him this way, but never the less it to was part of the loss. Yes, a settlement everyone had to live with, but not without losses. Would any settlement be large enough to undo the damage that was done to these two? Money could never fix all of the damage. Nothing could. Time would help, but the damage was done. Jory was aware of the fact, but didn't like to give much thought to how sad she had become, but yet was unable to express any sadness through tears or crying. She couldn't cry anymore. It was another foreign feeling that had transpired, but there weren't any tears to cry. She didn't have the time or the energy to worry about how serious this probably was. What could it mean to feel so bad and to not be able to cry? She continuously heard the words in her mind over and over by Elton John's song, "Hard Done by You." It didn't matter who "YOU" was, but "hard" had been done. From this entire experience, her trust in Mason had been tested and shaken, but it did, however, remain. It was now stronger than ever. She knew there couldn't be a harder test, unless to lose Mason by death.

Jay and Todd were anticipating every detail that was needed to end the case. They, too, wanted it all to end. They had bigger, richer clients awaiting their services. All papers would be signed immediately with a check for two million dollars to be delivered to Mason. It was money remitted for his new freedom, his returned freedom. Looking over the past years, two million would never help explain the legal system, or eliminate the pain, but it did reinforce and explain reality, that money was the guiding force in society. This was it. Take it. Move on. Don't look back. This was reality. Born innocence—gone. Every day and every minute in this society provided opportunity for thieves to prey on the innocent. They were on the backs of the innocent, the naive. The trick was to keep them at ones back because they do exist and are everywhere. The truth was that Mason did get paid two million dollars for his and only his invention. That fact did feel good. After all, anyone can steal, but very few can create—and to do it so brilliantly. Yes, this is what Mason and Jory would hold on to. Not that criminals could beat the system up one side and down the other, walk into the Secretary of State office and simply ask to change the President's/Owner's name of the company without any questions asked and to destroy innocent peoples lives to line their own pockets with money that did not belong to them. What is this system we call a judicial system? After all, a president can be impeached and not be removed from office. A football star can slice up his ex-wife and walk away a millionaire. What a country. What a society.

For this anniversary, or perhaps to celebrate their regained freedom, Mason had purchased two tickets to Paris to recuperate. Both were limited in excitement, mainly due to exhaustion and shock and the repetition of bad feelings that were like a bad rerun playing daily. Jory often compared the lawsuit to the movie, *Groundhog Day*. Every day playing the exact same routine, but certainly not equal in comedy.

On the morning of May 31st, it was a new movie. Mason and Jory loaded the Trooper with luggage. The vehicle was literally packed full enough to cause a bulging like an obese belly that just consumed a thanksgiving dinner. Jory delivered Hobbes to the next door neighbor, Lovee Lowe. Lovee, a lovely little German lady name Beulah Lovee Lowe, was known to everyone as "Lovee." Her name was given to her to signify her beauty, which it did so well. If a name could be so exact for a person, Lovee's was. She was a tiny, white-haired, ninety-three-year-old and a friend to everyone and especially to Hobbes. The feeling was mutual. She barely stood five feet tall and maybe on a good day weighed a hundred pounds. She talked with animated expression that was immeasurable and was as lovable as humanly possible. She was sharp as a tack and talking to her was a gift and knowing her, a privilege. She had much wisdom and so much to offer. Hobbes loved Lovee and if he couldn't be part of the activities with Mason or Jory then this was the next best place to be. Lovee used her German heritage to speak to Hobbes making him bilingual. Lovee always referred to Hobbes as her "Liebchen" meaning "sweetheart." Lovee had strict rules for Hobbes and she made him follow her "wules and wegulations." Mason and Jory had played, hugged, and showered Hobbes with love before they left. Hobbes always knew when Mason and Jory were leaving and if a dog could be bummed out, Hobbes did it every time. Today was different. Even Hobbes knew to let them go recuperate. He let out a big sigh, as he often did as a person would, and the liebchen ran to Lovee with tail-a-wagging.

Jory whispered, "I love you, my little guardian angel." She realized her behavior to this dog and was embarrassed by the fact that it was as hard for her to leave her Golden Retriever as it was for most people to leave their children. After all, Hobbes was practically like their child, and definitely was their best friend.

The two returned from Lovee's to their driveway and whimsically jumped into the Trooper. Mason tried to start the Trooper, but nothing happened. It was seven a.m. and the flight was at ten a.m. The drive to the airport took two hours. Both looked at each other and Jory said, "I thought our luck was supposed to be changing?"

Mason said, "Don't worry, it's just the battery. We can jump it and still make it!" With a warm smile, he said gently, "Don't expect miracles, it will take time to get our luck back. It will come back, Jory."

As Mason was handling the details at hand, Jory was remembering a backpacking vacation they had both taken a few years earlier in the rugged terrain of Colorado. It was the first of many backpacking trips they took. Jory put on pounds and pounds of gear. Before hiking four miles straight up, Mason strapped the gear to Jory as she laughed and fell backwards, feet straight up. Unfortunately, he was serious and she did indeed manage, with difficulty. However, after four hours UP, she was practically dying or thought she was and knew she couldn't go any further. She remembered Mason saying, "it's just right up over the hill!" Believing him, she regained strength to carry on only to find that up the hill was another humongous rockslide—big, bad and hard. Of course, the two eventually made it. Through all of it, it had become a joke when there was a hard task, one of them would say, "just one more rock slide."

As Mason was fixing the lifeless Trooper she mumbled, "Just one more rock slide."

"I heard that Jory and, no, it's not a rock slide," Mason rumbled. His sense of humor was a tad out of alignment these days. Both were snarling to some degree as the Trooper interrupted the tense moment, with the engine humming. This humming was music to their ears.

Mason and Jory made it to the airport to watch their plane take off. With great disappointment, Mason went to the ticket counter and with minimal hassles and damage, the trip would continue. All their flights were off by just one time slot. Ironically, Mason and Jory arrived in New York early enough to get on their original flight—TWA Flight 800. With all things off a tad, they decided to just take their new, later, flights that were given to them in Kansas City and keep the hassles to a minimum. This was very important for them to do these days.

"Flight 800 to Paris, France now boarding at gate 31A," they heard in the background. Mason and Jory had made themselves comfortable. Mason was eating some chocolate ice cream and Jory writing the book she always wanted to write. She saw the opportunity books brought in allowing experiences to be felt and lessons to be learned. The urge to write was always there, but she never felt she had anything interesting to write about until now. Boy, did she have a story to tell and she knew she could do it because she had the intimate knowledge, first hand knowledge of what it took to survive. First hand experience of inventing and developing an organization herself. A type of, *How to Survive Manual*—so to speak. Both were content for the moment. The area emptied, providing a much needed space, whether it was legitimate or just, "much needed space." Hundreds of passengers boarded the plane. Mason's eyes were fixed on a tiny, dark-haired, child. His dark curls looked like silk, and soft almost to the point of looking like fake hair of a doll. That's what he was, a doll. He was so adorable and full of life. He acted as if he was an Eveready Bunny disguised as a little boy, so energetic and no signs of energy declining anytime soon. He was obviously ready for his trip. He boarded the plane with his mother who was gripping toys in one hand and the tiny little warm hand in the other. Mason stretched out over a couple of chairs, as their next flight wasn't for forty minutes. Both sat there in a trance. Neither of them were used to not having to worry about losing everything they had ever worked for or been. It had become the familiar. As both of them were relaxing, eight minutes of vegging out had gone by. Jory, staring into space, was slapped out of her trance with a huge ball of fire seen in the air. The pane glass windows shattered. Mason jumped up and ran as close as he could to the shattered glass. "Oh, my God!" both quietly uttered. The airport grew silent momentarily and spontaneously turned into complete havoc. The ball of fire was huge! It was sending millions of descending, firework appendages down into the Atlantic Ocean.

Eventually, an announcement came over the PA system as everyone in the area stood glued to the scene, "We have just received word that TWA Flight 800 to Paris exploded over the Atlantic Ocean." The NTSB and rescue crews were immediately on the scene to search for survivors. Mason and Jory looked at each other, knowing there could be no survivors. Tears filling both, both trembling, they grabbed and held each other in a lock that could never separate them. Rumors immediately started flying about bombs, terrorists, explosions, and the like, destroying Flight 800.

Mason continued to tremble and continued holding Jory. He whispered in her ear, "Jory, our luck just changed."

Jory pulled slightly away from Mason and looked into his tear-filled eyes. "Mason, please, my God, please tell me it is irony that we were supposed to be on that plane?"

As she said the last word, Mason put his finger over her mouth and insisted, "Shhhhh, honey, don't think that." After a few minutes of trying to grasp this horrifying incident, Mason made a phone call to family to let them know that he and Jory were alive. *Then* he decided to be on the *safe* side and make a call to Jay, too.

THE END

Printed in the United States
70151LV00002B/179